# THE ROBOT'S HEART

## TORIA'S STORY

MARIA P FRINO

MPG COMMUNICATIONS

The Robot's Heart: Toria's Story



First edition



This is a work of fiction.

Author: Maria P. Frino

Cover Design: Mark Drolc, Graphic Designer

Visit the author's website – www.mariapfrino.com

All inquiries should be made to the author – mariapfrino@gmail.com

ISBN: 9780648894650

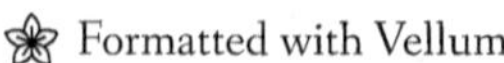
Formatted with Vellum

*To all my readers*
*Thanks for appreciating my stories*

# ONE

## When Two TRAIs Meet

LIGHT FLICKERS from the television screen in my designated home in the TRAI community compound. Yet another story about the ineffectiveness of me and my team of TRAI robots in attracting the human terrorists who live in their enclaves in The Second Zone, an area towards the arid outback. We are meant to bring them to justice, bring them back here to Harbour City, my home.

My auditory... I mean my ears, detect the human speaking on the screen. After many years of dealing with humans, I sometimes forget I can speak and think in their voice, rather than the inbuilt robotic one assigned to me.

These media stories, of which there have been many, are music to the terrorists' ears. We TRAI – *Terror Response Attraction Igoids* (attraction robots), are failing in keeping terrorists at bay with some skirmishes happening close to the city walls in recent years. The terrorists are becoming brazen in their bid to overthrow the government of Harbour City and place us back into the dystopian years we endured during the war years of the late 2800s.

Wars were commonplace in the world even before I came along, but nothing compared to the devastation of the 20-year war.

I am not the only robot in the TRAI community to be causing issues with capturing terrorists, but I am ageing the fastest. And I am also the elder of thousands of TRAI the world over.

After oiling my joints, I stumble to the television, switching it off. Oiling is necessary as being the elder of the TRAI community, I must look after myself. Even though I'm creaking and have minor cracks in places, there is no need for me to be put on the scrap heap just yet. I have a few more years left in me yet, quite a few if I have my way.

Conscious of time, I ready myself to go to the Assembly Theatre, it's in the city centre. This is where TRAI - Terror Response Attraction Igoids (have I mentioned this already?), human-like robots like me, are created.

The city centre is close enough I don't need my aeromobile, it is only a 15-minute walk. In my early years as the newest TRAI, I could be there in 5-minutes, but alas much time has passed and my circuits know it.

My memory bank is flooded with victories from those early years, back in the 2880s when I came to be and through to this day. The numbers of terrorists I attracted, lured if you like, and brought to The Dungeon were in the thousands. Now, with my ageing circuits, I bumble my way through trying to attract one or two terrorists out of hiding. It is only due to me being the first TRAI built that I am still part of the team, I am a *'favoured one'* you might say. But I need to be careful, if I keep causing issues and not performing as I should, I won't be part of the team for much longer.

Arriving at the Assembly Theatre, I enter focusing on the humans clustered around a white surgical table, their lab coats stark under the overhead lights. They communicate in hushed tones, their voices muted to my ears. Secrecy in this room is paramount, it is only a few scientists who are privy to what is happening. What I do know is they are preparing another unit, an additional TRAI robot, an asset being built for operational efficiency. This robot will be an extension of my function in keeping humans of our city safe.

*And maybe a baby-sitter for me.*

I push this thought aside and focus on the reason I am here, to meet this latest TRAI.

The air is heavy with high concentrations of sterilisation agents and industrial-grade chemicals. My olfactory input registers them as harsh but non-disruptive. The scientists are busy working but one acknowledges me with a slight nod of his head. I register that he has seen me.

My system also registers the atmosphere as sterile in the controlled environment of the Assembly Theatre, which is to be expected. This is the designated facility where TRAI robots achieve operational status. *'Born'* is the human designation for this process. It is not technically accurate, yet I prefer that word to the term 'being built'. The word 'born' establishes a symbolic connection to the species we have been programmed and trained to protect.

The scientists pivot toward me. Their leader advances. Professor Hugh Nichols. He is the primary architect of the TRAI initiative, foremost authority in computational sciences. His voice remains steady, delivering information with precision. I process his words. The next sequence in my directive is imminent.

"Toria," Nichols states, his tone measured. "Are you prepared to meet your new partner?"

"Affirmative, Professor," I respond. "Proceed with the introduction." I was told about requiring a partner exactly one year ago. It was not a pleasant idea for me as I have managed this long in my leadership of the TRAI community. However, I am programmed to obey.

Behind Professor Nichols, a towering figure emerges - precise construction, optimised efficiency. His presence is evident. I pause momentarily to process.

"Toria, this is Travis," Nichols continues. "A TRAI unit calibrated to enhance your operational effectiveness. He is designed to complement your capabilities, better them and execute commands without deviation."

*Better them!* Ah, I guess this is necessary given my current capabilities. I step forward, initiating analysis. "Designation: TOR-1A, known as Toria," I state, extending my hand.

Travis does not reciprocate. Instead, he inclines his upper frame in a controlled bow. "Designation: TRA-150, known as Travis," he replies. "Function: Operational support. Status: Ready."

"Acknowledged, Travis." My optical sensors scan upward, assessing his structural dimensions. "Height differential detected." I redirect my attention to Professor Nichols. "My height specifications are above standard, was his scale increased for psychological effect?"

Professor Nichols emits a brief laugh. "No Toria, his proportions serve a tactical purpose, he is a disincentive to hostiles like the terrorists of The Second Zone. Your partnership is calculated for maximum enforcement efficiency."

This is the professor's way of saying I require help. My last few missions have not achieved optimal impact. I am not incapable of doing my job, however, my performance of late is less than adequate.

I return my focus to Travis. His stance remains neutral, yet micro-adjustments on his face suggest recognition of the exchange happening between us. "Understood, Professor," I state. "Initiating integration protocols. Travis will be introduced to the team and calibrated for mission deployment."

"Your confirmation is accepted," Nichols replies. "Ensure full system synchronisation. Efficiency is paramount."

"Execution will happen," I acknowledge, then turn to Travis. "Follow. Orientation sequence commencing."

# TWO

## The Orientation

I LEAD him through the main part of the Assembly Centre. Travis lumbers behind me, his movements floundering, almost as if he has imaginary roller skates on. He hasn't quite figured out how to navigate his sheer size and weight, and I'm starting to think he was assembled with two left feet. He is leaning forwards slightly, I'd call it a *slump*, and it's not a good look either, it's unbecoming of a TRAI. I mentally flag this for immediate correction. A robot must stand tall, command presence, exude intimidation! I certainly do ... well, in my head I do. Up until a couple of years ago, I did have a presence and was always in command, I was proud of my achievements in attracting terrorists.

We step into the common room, where off-duty TRAI robots gather to recharge and exchange their latest firmware gossip. There is silence as we enter. A great leader commands silence. I pretend it has nothing to do with the fact that last week I shut down this entire room's power by accident during an inspirational speech. Completing the speech, I gathered my laptop and headed to my seat. Only, as I moved, I tripped on a cord causing the blackout. They are still wary of me, watching me in case I stumble again.

"Fellow members," I declare with all the authority of a robotic overlord, "it is my honour to introduce our newest recruit, Designation: TRA-150, known as Travis. Please, welcome him warmly."

The response is as lukewarm as the recharging port at the back of the room. A few murmured greetings, some scattered nods, and one particularly unenthusiastic thumbs-up from a robot who is absolutely playing a game on his holo-screen instead of paying attention. Rude!

I'm not surprised the other TRAIs have little interest in Travis right now, this is break time and they are in relax mode. This will change once we're all out in the field doing our jobs. TRAI are built to be team members and perform their duties as trained. Their programming is absolute, they protect the citizens of Harbour City.

I turn to Travis, who is currently standing at an angle that suggests his joints have given up on him. "Take no notice of them," I say firmly. "They'll respect you once they witness your potential."

Travis meets my gaze, his optics flickering like he's processing a particularly difficult equation. "I have no interest in making friends," he states. "Their attitude is of no concern to me. I am here to be educated by you, capture terrorists, and serve the humans."

I nod with purpose, pretending I do not detect the faintest glitch in my circuits at how eerily similar he sounds to me in my youth. "Good," I say. "Your confirmation of protocols pleases me."

The other TRAI robots shift back into their previous activities, and I take a moment to bask in my own magnificence. Years of relentless effort, strategic planning, and unwavering dedication have brought me to this point: Head Robot of the TRAI community for twenty years straight. I am a beacon of robotic excellence. And, if I may say so myself, an icon of leadership.

"Now," I continue, placing a firm hand on Travis's shoulder, "the first thing we shall address is your atrocious posture."

Travis blinks. "I was constructed this way."

"Nonsense," I say. "A leader stands tall, exudes confidence, and moves with purpose." I demonstrate by striking my most authoritative pose, a stance so powerful it demands admiration.

That's when my foot catches on an exposed wire, and I plummet to the ground with all the grace of a toppled vending machine.

Laughter ensues from the team. Travis offers his hand to help me up, which I ignore.

I reboot my dignity, stand up, and dust myself off. "That," I announce, "was a test."

Travis tilts his head. "Of what?"

"... your ability to adapt to unexpected situations. You passed."

He nods solemnly. "Understood."

We take a seat across from each other, I pull my laptop toward me. "Let's get started." Travis will receive his laptop and other items over the next few days, he won't be needing them straight away.

With a few keystrokes, I bring up a detailed map of the facility. In the next tab is a two-hundred-page document chronicling our history, our mission, and the role he will play.

I turn the laptop so Travis can view the screen. "This," I say, meeting his eyes, "is where it all begins. Pay attention. You're not here to only assist, you're here joining me in making more of an impact."

# THREE

## The First Task

A WEEK LATER, on the first of the month, Travis accompanies me to The Dungeon. This day is significant because each month I have a meeting with Madame Secretary to discuss missions and their progress. It's the first time I have had to introduce a new TRAI to her. She knows of my failings and will be pleased to meet Travis, I'm sure.

This building where captured terrorists are housed is not actually a dungeon, it is a prison with underground cells of impenetrable steel cast rooms with the possibility of escape being zero. The real name of the building is 'Harbour City Penitentiary', the largest building of its kind in the southern hemisphere. It was built to house all of the citizens of Harbour City should another war ever happen. Every city around the world has their own version of this building.

The terrorists have never wanted the safe, authoritarian life the humans of Harbour City are living. They are against all of our values – living with compassion and trust, following the new world rules to keep peace, liaising with the other cities that are left after the wars, and our caring for the environment as well as each other. These terrorist enclaves were formed during the long worldwide wars of the last century, they are what is left of the angry and displaced humans, the ones who won't forget and forgive.

Back then humans were dealing with an overheating world, lack of clean water due to less rain, and food became scarce due to soil degradation without the rain. The 20-year war had an extreme impact on the environment and people, which had already been impacted by previous wars. Some people became angry and riots started, small at first, but eventually leading to the worst world war. It was inevitable that terrorist gangs were formed.

Terrorist enclaves have been operational and growing for years. They cause sudden outbreaks of havoc and destruction wherever they exist throughout the world. Many of the cities have problems with them, some regional areas are spared.

Generally, they want power, power to rule in dystopian ways no one else wants. They started their brutal and horrific missions with the riots and have kept them up despite the rest of the world living in relative peace. Rumours abound of terrorists forming these clans during and after the wars of the 2800s when the world economy crashed and global warming had reached its peak. Anarchy prevailed at that time making the situation ideal for recruiting the displaced. These are the key reasons TRAI robots exist.

Today, many of the younger terrorists probably don't even know why they are still fighting, their elders are filling their minds with angry stories about the evil leaders who rule the few cities left on earth.

The environment was the biggest loser after the wars ended. It was destroyed by massive fires, billions of trees never grew back and any animals who were left had to adapt to the harsher environs. Mutations happened and many of these animals survive now in arid areas where humans cannot live.

We enter the building and our credentials are checked by the system, "Please enter Toria and Travis." The computer-generated robotic voice gives me chills, it has a Big Brother-esque vibe and it disrupts my systems every time I visit. This is unfathomable as I am a robot myself and I deal with the scum of human filth. Evil people hell-bent on destroying the human way of life and our TRAI community, so why does this voice bother me? The older I am, the more this voice aggravates me. I try not to allow this fear of authority take over, why would a robot fear authority?

This penitentiary also has an all-encompassing data system recording_every movement throughout Harbour City and environs. This control over all citizens, human and TRAI, means everyone is monitored. My concern is my last few missions, which were failures, were all captured and stored as data. I must improve because this is data that is frowned upon, a record of my failings.

The steel door rises revealing the massive foyer of offices housing the elite task force of humans who allocate our assignments and rule over all citizens. I motion Travis towards Door One allowing him to bow his head as he precedes me. The door closes automatically as I stand next to him in front of a massive desk of polished stainless steel taking up the length of the room.

Timber desks no longer exist. In fact, anything made

from timber only exists in a museum overseas, so I've been told. The trees and plants we have now are precious, no one would dare chop down a tree or destroy a plant. Even the terrorists abide by this rule in The Second Zone, they need the shelter the trees provide.

Standing rigidly to attention, we wait for the woman behind the desk to look up. The digital clock behind her clicks in the silence, it glows 0900 hours with the date below it – 01 February 3035.

When our highest-ranking official finally looks up, she acknowledges our rigid posture, then welcomes us to step further into her office.

"Ah Toria, welcome. And this is?" My sensors take in a woman of high status, hair coifed in a bun atop her head, enough make-up to enhance her face of forty years, her uniform of pants suit in mandatory black fitted to her generous frame.

"Thank you Madame Secretary, this is our newest recruit, known as Travis," I inform her. He bows and repeats what he said to me when we met, "Designation: TRA-150, Travis. Function: Operational support. Status: Ready."

"Hmm, formal isn't he?" she smiles her eyes still on me. "Ok then, you will continue your assignment to scout The Second Zone of Harbour City, the outskirts are where you will find terrorist enclaves, the elder terrorists are recruiting as we speak."

"I am familiar with this zone. As you know Madame Secretary, I have attracted and brought in many terrorists from there."

"Yes, I understand you have, Toria, which is why we are sending you back with Travis, he will learn much from you and your methods. It is imperative the TRAI initiative continues despite current sentiment amongst certain humans."

With this I stand a little taller, receiving recognition of my work pleases me. It is rare now, what with my recent failures. But ridding The Second Zone of the terrorist scum is my duty, it is the duty of all TRAI robots. The citizens of our capital city expect to go about their daily routine in safety.

LATER, we are in the armoury where the tools of our trade are held. My arms and legs are my weapons, they are filled with blades and bullets ready to be actioned if necessary. As I wait for Travis to be fitted with chest, back and arm armour, I think about my new partner. He will need to stand up to the pressure. Will the terrorists be intimidated by him, and will he be an asset or a hindrance? The last thing I need is to be hindered, I can hinder myself quite well on my own these days.

When we are ready, I ask Travis to follow me through the secret back entrance of The Dungeon, the safest place in this building. It is the humungous hallway leading to the backdoor, a fortress of titanium steel double the thickness of the rest of this building. In case of a nuclear attack or another war, all the elite members of Harbour City will be ushered into this area with another area next to it to house the millions of citizens. Ironically, the other safest area is where the terrorists are housed. Once a terrorist is sentenced to life here, this is where they stay.

A heavily armoured aeromobile hovers outside, waiting for us. The sky is thick with smog, the air heavy with pollution, which is worse than usual today. I can't remember the last time the sun broke through the murky haze over

Harbour City. Despite strict environmental laws, the damage lingers, a stubborn scar on the city's skyline. Environmental scientists are scrambling to assist Mother Nature in improving air quality, but the wars left humans with major climate change issues.

I ask Travis to sit in the passenger side of the vehicle and wait patiently as he squeezes himself into the seat, he bends his head to fit.

"Comfortable?"

"Negative."

"We don't have too far to go," I lie. The Second Zone is the furthest outpost of our country, we have a two-hour flight. Being uncomfortable won't help Travis to relax.

He speaks again. "I detect engine issues. This aeromobile requires maintenance."

I don't bother answering, many of the TRAI assets are in need of maintenance, some urgent. Much like me, they have been overlooked due to budget constraints and lack of staff. Scientists are trying to keep the TRAI community going with a limited budget and this, at least in my opinion, is the reason our efficiency is lacking. Travis will help me but we need more like him to help the rest of the ageing team. However, this is unlikely as funds to build more TRAIs don't exist, we will need to perform with the team we have.

It has been some years now that I have not measured up. Professor Nichols is ageing too, he no longer commands the respect he once had. Travis is his last build. Every time I encounter the Professor now, his blond locks are thinned and tinged greyer, his once bright green eyes are muted, and his once taut body is soft. He finds it difficult to stand tall.

We have had many conversations about his deteriorating memory and how he is no longer able to teach other scientists to build TRAI robots. But then, some scientists are no longer interested in what is now seen as outdated AI technology. And Harbour City lacks the funds to keep such a facility thriving. Professor Nichols still advocates we TRAI are needed because who else is there to protect the citizens? And no citizen wants to enter The Second Zone unless they want to be a terrorist.

Terrorists flock to The Second Zone and other places like it in the world. The one we are headed to is at the edge of the arid centre, inhospitable unless you are willing to live this lifestyle. The heat, the dust and the feral animals keep law-abiding humans away. Living there, you take your life in your own hands against the venomous snakes, spiders, crawling and airborne insects, and mutated ferals. Then there are the giant cicadas, the size of mice, with their incessant buzzing and clicking sounds so loud they are dangerous to human ears. And yet, in these harsh surroundings, the terrorists have contrived to set up a sophisticated recruitment and training network. They have become immune to the cicadas song.

As a TRAI, history is taught only to provide context, the elements necessary for our functioning. We learn of the protracted wars that polluted the rivers and inevitably the ocean. During the 20-year war so many toxic chemicals were used as weapons. Of course, the stronger humans adapted and survived. Harbour City is one of the few larger cities in the whole world that seems to be surviving well. London, now known as Thames City, is another. Most cities were renamed after the wars due to the population being severely depleted and survivors wanting to leave the past behind.

As I pilot the aeromobile, I explain to Travis about my unique ability. Unlike other TRAI units, I am equipped with a mind-manipulation capability allowing me to extract critical information from the most hardened criminals. With this ability, I can uncover the location of terrorist enclaves, their plans, and even their intended targets. This is in addition to my attraction methods used to bring terrorists out of hiding.

Professor Nichols and his team have frequently been among those targeted, making my skill invaluable in protecting them and others. What I don't tell Travis is that this skill is impaired due to my ageing systems and it is for this reason Travis exists. He will help when I stumble and my skills do not attract the terrorists as they once did.

This mind-bending ability is exclusive to me, a trait no other TRAI robot shares. Why I alone possess it remains a mystery, though it was a source of pride to use it effectively in my work safeguarding humanity. Unfortunately, there are limits to this power, and not only because of my growing impairment. Some of the most dangerous terrorist leaders are shielded by radicalised robots who were captured and reprogrammed to serve the terrorists' agenda. These robotic protectors make direct access to such leaders nearly impossible, presenting a unique challenge in our missions.

# FOUR

## The Second Zone

WE ARRIVE at the Zone with me helping Travis out of the aeromobile, his joints having stiffened during our flight.

"You lied."

"Apologies for the deception, I didn't want you to focus on how uncomfortable you were. Now please straighten up, we have terrorists to capture."

Suddenly, a scraping noise pierces the misty surrounds. My sensors have been on high alert since we landed. "Show yourself," I command, bracing for an attack. Travis straightens beside me, his stance mirroring the drills I have drummed into him.

"Disgusting. My olfactory sensors are red lining from the stench."

"Oh, the smell? You'll get used to it one day." Another lie. A big one. I guess I'm trying to ease him into the discomfort of working in The Second Zone. Confession - on every mission, this smell assails me. The stench is a horrifying cocktail of rotting vegetation, decomposing flesh, faeces, and whatever toxic sludge the terrorists still use to keep their enemies at bay. No one ever gets used to it.

The cicadas are in full swing too. "How do the terrorists stand these blaring noises? And others who venture out here?"

"That is a conundrum, Travis. I have been told they become used to the sound, many terrorists claiming they hear it even while in The Dungeon. It is a lingering buzz. It is the same for other humans, they become accustomed to it. Although, hearing loss becomes a problem with prolonged stays here. You will notice many terrorists have hearing problems.

Footsteps echo in the distance. First walking. Then running.

"Stop. Halt, I say!" I'm yelling, not that it matters. As if that's ever worked on a fleeing suspect.

We head down the bush path following the footsteps. The putrid stench launches an assault on our senses as we go deeper into the bush. In the overgrown shadows, I catch sight of a small figure darting ahead of us. With a gesture, I signal Travis to take the lead while I slip into a smaller path to cut him off. Stumbling through rubble, I pause. Silence. Great. Now I've lost him.

Then - bam!

A small figure slams into me, and I hit the ground hard. A filthy concrete and tangled roots, rotting leaves and twigs welcome mat.

Dazed, I blink up to see a child scrambling backward, peddling away like an injured crab.

"Stop! We just want to talk. We're not here to hurt you!" I say, hands raised.

Judging by his wide-eyed stare, he doesn't believe me.

Can't say I blame him, if a gigantic robot tackled me out of the darkness into a pile of trash, I wouldn't believe them either.

The child comes to a stop when Travis arrives, his huge feet a hindrance to the child going any further. Travis bends down pulling him up from his underarms. The child is kicking furiously but it's no use, Travis has him up near his shoulders, lifted metres in the air.

"Calm yourself. I am Toria and this is Travis, we only want to ask a few questions. Where is your clan and are you able to take us to them?"

"No. Why would I do that? So you can drag us all into The Dungeon?" He has stopped kicking now, obviously he has realised how futile it is to fight.

"Only if they are terrorists. Are they?" The child hangs limp in Travis' grip, so I continue. "What devious plans do they have to hurt our humans?"

"I was out scouting for food." The answer is childishly simple, direct. I recognise I'm unlikely to get any useful intelligence from him.

It is unusual to see one so young on their own. "You were out on your own? Then you are not part of a clan." As I say this, Travis, who has also been on watch, indicates others are heading our way. I hear the thunder of footsteps heading towards us.

"We need to leave here now." The child has suddenly lost his bravado and tells us to hide in the scrub. "They will kill me and destroy both of you."

He is telling me what I already know.

We obey, me a little hesitant at first because he is a child, but he is a human and our programming compels us to follow all human orders. The child's fear pulses through the air as the sound of heavy footsteps grows closer, their echo bouncing off the bush landscape. The terrorists' voices cut through the silence, sharp and furious: "Where are you? We know you took our weapons!"

My circuits hum with tension as they close in, their shouts ringing in my sensors. The boy shakes, his eyes wide with fear. For an agonising moment they are close, but then, they thunder past, their heavy boots crunching through the arid bush and scrub, heading further into the desolation.

We remain frozen, the weight of their proximity pressing down on us like a storm breaking loud and strong. Then their sounds lessen, they have gone deeper into the arid region.

Travis is now holding the boy on his hip with both of the child's hands restrained. Does he think the boy is going to attack him? Not likely, I can see the boy's fear, his eyes glisten with unshed tears. He is trying not to show his feelings.

I appease his fear. "Thank you, there could have been an altercation, their marching indicated their anger. Did you steal some of their weapons?"

"Why should I tell you?"

"Because we can assist you, it is not safe for you to stay here if you have stolen something belonging to the terrorists. You know they won't stop hunting you."

The child remains quiet, his head hanging. My sensors quieten, I begin to sense his reticence making me feel something ... what is happening? We robots are not programmed to feel emotion, but with years of protecting humans, my sensors have developed a soft spot for them, especially children. This one may be twelve or thirteen, he is filthy and his clothes hang off him, who knows when he last ate?

# FIVE

## The Child's Lair

AFTER CONVINCING the child no good was to come from him fighting us, he has taken us to his *'home'*, a derelict shed where he can live out of the elements. This is where he had stored the few bits of armour he had stolen.

Still, the danger from the ferals is close too, something to be wary of. This, along with the terrorists makes this area dangerous for all. The drone of the cicadas is also constant, the height of summer is when they are at their loudest.

"Stealing is a crime even if it is from other criminals. You are in danger."

"I have to protect myself, I only took what I am able to use. The terrorists have many other weapons."

Again, I feel another human emotion, that of sadness. This boy is lost and I ask him how he came to be here. He tells us his father was part of a terrorist clan, a group that did not agree with what the main clans wanted to do.

"My father tried to reason with them that we could

negotiate with Madame Secretary and her government to bring these times to peace, he was sick of being on the run and constantly fearing for our lives. He along with my mother, one of my brothers and my little sister were murdered while I was out finding food with my older brother, Evan. It wasn't enough to lose the others, Evan died last month from malnutrition, he gave me most of what we collected. What little we did find, he gave me the bigger portion."

This poor boy is all alone and I see the emotion on his face, emotions one so young should not yet feel. This is my advantage, it won't be hard to convince him to come with us. "We will stay here tonight, Travis will go to find food for you. Tomorrow you will come with us to the city, I promise you we will get you the help you need. On your own here, you will perish."

He stands on the bare earth, shoeless and helpless. "I know you are a TRAI and are programmed to protect humans, but why protect me, what worth am I to you?"

"You seem to have been abandoned by the rest of your clan. Should they not have stepped up and looked after you?"

"Maybe they would have, but no one came looking for me. I guess they had enough to deal with, having their own children to care for. It's tough to feed hungry mouths, why would they want another one?"

A sadness creeps over me again. I do not know why these feelings are happening, but this boy is vulnerable and I have a need to care for him.

Travis had already left to find food so it is only the two of us. My sensors flood with affection towards the boy. Is this love? I must do more research, find out more about why I am feeling such emotions.

"Every human life is precious, even yours. You are young, you have the chance to live a full life if you trust us. Contrary to the rumours you may have heard, I am not as brutal as some say." The terrorists I have had sentenced spread rumours about how ruthless I am at attracting them with my power and convincing them I will help to deradicalise them, giving them a better life. All I am doing is my job, I am not ruthless.

"Toria, I thought I had heard that name. So you're the one who strikes fear in the clans."

"That is the rumour, yes. Are you scared of me?"

"Not now. I was when you were both chasing me."

We stand in silence for some time until we hear Travis return. He has an apple and some stale bread for the child.

We stand and watch him devour the food. He then lies down amongst the filth of the dirty mattress and sleeps.

I indicate to Travis to follow me towards the outskirts, only a few minutes' walk away from where the boy sleeps. We stand and listen as the nocturnal ferals awaken. The hissing, snarling and growling is unsettling.

"Thanks for your help today, you are a fast learner."

"I was built to obey, there is no need to thank me."

We stand quietly together for a few more minutes and then move away from the ferals' sounds back to the boy's home. It is time for us to each take turns in powering down for the night. One of us must stand guard in case of an ambush and I am determined to protect this boy.

The next morning we are on our way back to Harbour City with him. My protection senses are on high alert, no one is going to harm this child if I have anything to do with it. He has been through enough with losing his family in such a brutal way.

# SIX

Toria

3037

THE CHILD'S name is Mannix. Since Travis and I brought him to Harbour City in 3035, he has lived near the TRAI facility. He befriended my team, as did Travis eventually. We are like a family, we protect Mannix.

I had taken Mannix to meet Madame Secretary once he had some meat on his bones and looked more respectable. This had taken a few months of him eating well and sleeping the regular hours a teenager requires.

Madame Secretary had listened to his story and how his family had been murdered. She had asked if he would be able to identify the murderers who were probably already in The Dungeon. Mannix was willing to try, his anger at what happened to his family had kept him alive in those dangerous parts of the Second Zone.

Unfortunately, he was not able to identify those who murdered his family, so this may not go any further. To what end? Looking for the terrorists who killed Mannix's family is like looking for ghosts in the wasteland.

When I look at Mannix, I see a human who can make change happen and help us to rid the world of the terrorist scum the TRAI community and all humans despise. He knows the ways of the terrorists and their brutal minds more than anyone in Harbour City.

We teach Mannix martial arts, show him how to use our sophisticated weaponry, teach him to box, and show him how to meditate to gain strength. He grows into a powerful teenager in front of our eyes.

Mannix is slowly finding powers he didn't know he possessed. At sixteen, he is growing into a man, puberty has him looking and feeling more masculine. He has a unique smell, a mix of a muskiness and sweaty nervousness.

The children of the humans who work with Madame Secretary were wary of him at first. It was curiosity rather than fear. He has a few friends now, but Mannix concentrates on becoming a warrior, a team member of the TRAI community. This is something he wants rather than us just giving him this task.

His power? He has the same ability I have, he can manipulate minds. We discovered this during a training session, Mannix was able to manipulate his boxing trainer to give him more tasks even though his trainer thought he wasn't ready. After his session, his trainer had told me what happened.

I find him in the Common Room.

"I understand you did something extraordinary in training today?"

Mannix had finished stuffing his face with food and is wiping his mouth. "Did I?" His smile warmed my sensors, my chest is full of pride. If this is what a full heart feels like, then I have one.

"So, you have the same power I do."

"Apparently. I didn't even realise I was doing it until my trainer told me. He asked how I did it."

"We will work on you being able to harness this power to use when necessary. It will take time."

He smiled again. It's a smile so familiar to me now.

He excused himself from the table, "I need to shower and go to the recovery room. My muscles ache with all the extra training I've done."

I watched as he walked out of the common room, the power this child has over me is overwhelming, my sensors are full of things no robot should feel. I stood there for some time wondering what else this young human is going to give us.

I am determined to protect Mannix in ways I have not wanted to protect any other human, he is my number one priority. No one will harm him while I am around.

# SEVEN

## The Missions Continue

MORE TRAI ARE DEPLOYED to the Second Zone, some will stay for months if necessary.

Travis and I return to the Zone often. One particular day, I learn just how much I need Travis by my side.

We find ourselves in the same spot where we found Mannix. We were careful and thought we had our senses on alert, but then suddenly find a group of terrorists were surrounding us, hemming in us. What the hell?

I realise then our attraction sensors were disrupted when an AI-assisted brain app was used by the terrorists to scramble our systems. Our abilities were muted and we tried valiantly to save us from capture, which was as effective as paper umbrellas in a hurricane. My arms were lead weights rendering them useless, although Travis seemed to be faring better than me.

Travis is unable to help as he is accosted by six of the terrorists and bound with ropes. We are crouched on the disgusting path, the terrorists discussing how to bring us to their headquarters. Their backs to us, Travis whispers, "I have an idea."

Suddenly, the ropes holding Travis catch fire and he throws them towards the terrorists. They scream as their skin sizzles. Travis stands lifting me in his arms as he runs back towards our aeromobile. The screams become muted as the distance between us grows.

Travis places me gently in the passenger seat. "I will drive, you are not fit." I begin to protest ... "When we return to Harbour City, the professor's team can work on your circuits. The AI equipment the terrorists use is efficient. You were in grave danger."

"You were too. But how... where did the fire come from?"

Travis shows me his awkward smile, he has no human traits at all. I am the queen of those, I guess. "You are not the only robot to have special powers."

I remain silent thanking the professor for his insight in me requiring a partner.

The Professor's team worked on my circuits giving me my strength back. When we had told them about the AI app, they forge together in creating another app to counter this, one we can use against them.

MANNIX HAS BEEN quiet as he is busy with his training. I visit him in his rooms. Finding him on his holo-screen playing a game, it pleases me to see him relaxing.

"Give me one sec... there I'm done. Hi Toria." I notice his high score before he powers down. Clever boy.

"Hello Mannix, you've been a stranger, we have missed

your presence in the common room." I stand near his front door, waiting for an invitation to sit with him.

"No reason, busy training and discovering some other powers. Enter, what are you waiting for?"

"Interesting. Want to enlighten me?"

"Turns out I have magical powers, I am part of The Enchantment Community, have you heard of them?"

I nod indicating I had heard of this community of people with magical powers who were close to being eradicated during the wars.

"This includes the mind-bending one you possess. I have been perfecting these powers."

I am stunned into silence. This is amazing, this young boy may be a prodigy, there is more to Mannix than we first thought. I was right to think he was going to give us more.

"Well, do you want to hear about it all?" He takes my silence as disinterest, which it is clearly not. He raises his hand towards a chair indicating I sit.

I move and sit with him at his round dining table, small yet enough for two people. His quarters are tiny, but he has never complained.

"It is best we go and visit Madame Secretary, she will be extremely interested in your news." People who possess magical powers, Enchanters as you call them, have been scarce since the 2880s when many were wiped out."

"Sure, whenever you're ready." His manner is nonchalant, as if what he has just informed me of is of no consequence. How wrong can he be? This is huge and an even huger weapon against terrorists.

TRAVIS and I keep up with our missions. We are back in

the Second Zone months after the AI mishap with our team of TRAI helping us.

The scientists had come up with a fix in case the terrorists tried the brain app again. Our TRAI brains are now immune to such attacks. This technology was shared with other scientists around the world, the first time in years that our systems had been enhanced. What little funds we have left had been put to good use. Everything helps in our quest to eradicate this threat to our peaceful lives.

We take the terrorist clans by surprise, using stealth in the moonless night to ambush them. It was nice to see there were no women and children around. Only adult men and their young counterparts, many of them fit and able. Also, the radicalised TRAI were ready for us. Had they known of an upcoming attack by us?

We fight with all of our means, the younger terrorists along with the terrorist TRAI were a force we were not expecting. What we thought was going to be a short mission ended up being longer than anticipated.

"Back up required. Terrorists ready to be transported to Harbour City." By the fifth day, we managed to bring them down, but we had our own casualties too. A quarter of our TRAI team were wounded, some completely destroyed by the chemical weaponry these humans still used even though they had been long banned.

"Copy that, deploying transport," comes the instant reply from one of our team.

I place my transcoder that doubles as a phone, back into its charger in the aeromobile. Travis is sitting in the driver's seat ready to depart.

"Give me a few minutes to check if there are others lurking about." He nods blankly. Is he tired? This has been a long mission but his circuits should be fine. I place in my memory bank a reminder to have him checked out.

As I walk past the assemblage of terrorists bound together on the ground ready to be transported, they hurl abuse towards me. "You're a crap excuse for a robot." "You will pay for this." "Bumbling fool robot can't do without her sidekick." "You're in danger of becoming extinct, Toria."

This last comment stings a little. I know I will no longer exist one day, but my worry is will the TRAI community still exist. Maybe this haul of scum we captured will perk peoples' interest in our community again, there are more than fifty in this group.

As I walk away they are hauled into the Dungeon jet. They all belong in The Dungeon. I park another reminder to alert the media about this successful mission. Journalists have been reporting on these TRAI missions since the beginning, years of stories, some good, some not so good.

I am near the outskirts taking in the red dirt, the heat and the scurrying insects as behind me I hear the roar of the jets departing for The Dungeon. The terrorists' homes are silent, it seems we have captured all of them who had remained here to protect their territory. This is a type of hell no human can endure but yet the terrorists have made it their home. They have skills in making their homes cool by building them into the southern sides of the sand dunes, they manufacture a form of electricity from water found deep in the ground. They use AI to their advantage, the only thing keeping the clans together. Their internal struggles are well-known.

As I head back to where Travis is, I hear noises to my left. Flagging I am on my own, I still decide to investigate and bending down, I peak my head through the bushes. A boulder hits me with force, I crash to the ground.

I feel myself being dragged, somewhere. Then I vaguely hear voices, two I think.

"Drag her here next to this tree. I'll run home."

I'm waking up slowly, my circuits trying to unscramble. There is a child standing in front of me, staring. "Wha ..." I try my attraction systems but they're not working. My head isn't able to summon my mind-bending power, I struggle to read her mind. "You're a bit young to be out here on your own, aren't you?"

"I'm old enough. Now, shut it. The others will be here soon to take you to headquarters."

Ok, that is not going to happen. The last place I want to be is at another of the terrorists' hideouts on my own. With difficulty, I send a telepathic message to Travis hoping he understands it and can work out my coordinates. My head is frazzled but hopefully not too much that the message doesn't get through.

Closing my eyes to try and restore power, I hear footsteps.

"Good job, Kara." A lithe man with sparse hair and mean, grey eyes, probably her father, pats her head. "You two, grab her feet and drag her to headquarters. Our leaders will be pleased to see her."

I'm struggling to conjure my mind-manipulating powers to read his thoughts and to send messages to Travis about where I'm being taken. My eyes are still closed as I try to restore my powers.

Then fireballs stream overhead, Travis is here somewhere.

One fireball connects with the man, his piercing scream is matched by his daughter's. The two holding my legs go to help their leader, throwing dirt and rubble to douse the fire.

Travis is next to me. "Come on, we need to leave."

Like I need to be told.

Back in the aeromobile, he is silent concentrating on his task of getting us home.

"You let me go out there again on my own. What were you thinking?"

"My circuits were in resting phase. Besides, I am trained to obey your orders. You asked me to stay with the others while you went out to check the scene again."

Did I? My memory circuits are failing me now, I thought I had asked Travis to follow me.

He's right, I guess, I should be more careful and check he is with me at all times. In the time since we rescued Mannix, he has saved me over and over. I must remember my limitations as an ageing robot, who when being reckless, is no good to anyone. "When you sense I am being stupid, I allow you to override that rule. Without you I would be in the terrorists clutches by now. This is information for you alone, no other TRAI, the Professor, or his team must know. Between us, ok?"

Travis bows his head slightly and I sense he is annoyed at my stupidity.

# EIGHT

Professor Hugh Nichols
2990

I SIGH as I enter my apartment. Toria is attracting attention with what is left of our world. Other countries are interested in my techniques and are willing to finance the making of more TRAI robots. Ten years after building Toria and a number of other TRAI, my invention is a hit. So, why am I so sad?

Terrorists have long been a hindrance in the world having peace. Since the wars of the 2800s, our world has had ecosystems and natural resources disrupted, which weakened our planet and many parts have been rendered unliveable. The cities remaining, thirty at last count, are under constant attack from terrorist clans wanting to take power. Harbour City is Australia's largest city and came from the remains of what was once Sydney. There are smaller regional areas here as well as in other countries who also need our help.

I'm sad because inventing Toria, although being a good thing, it may be too late. Will the planet recover from the damage humans have inflicted?

I pour myself a red wine and contemplate what has happened to date.

Crime prevention has become a high-stakes technological battlefield. Terrorist groups have evolved beyond detection while living in the far outskirts of Harbour City, the arid outback of what is left of Australia. Other cities have similar issues. The terrorists use advanced cloaking tech and AI-driven deception to evade capture. Conventional law enforcement struggles, and global security organisations are desperate for a breakthrough.

This is where I come in. Me, Professor Hugh Nichols, a genius in robotics and behavioural artificial intelligence (AI) and known for my controversial theories on predictive criminal behaviour. I was well beyond my years in this field, the youngest scientist in the team. Working in the classified labs of Harbour City, I believed that to catch the most dangerous minds, you needed a lure, something they couldn't resist.

Toria became my first robot. The breakthrough came when I combined three key technologies giving her powers to attract terrorists:

**Facial Recognition & Object Detection** – To identify threats from terrorists and remove ammunition and objects that may cause harm. This technology has been in use for years and many of the initial issues with it have been fixed.

**Neural Pattern Attraction System (NPAS)** – A cutting-edge algorithm that could analyse vast amounts of psychological and behavioural data to predict terrorist intent. Using this, a robot such as Toria can distract information from them.

**Quantum Justice Core (QJC)** – A self-learning AI processor capable of assessing a suspect's actions in real time, then by using the attraction system, robots are able to apprehend them.

This was the height of AI technology and helped to make me a leader in my field.

I programmed Toria to be more than a hunter; she was a temptation. Once engaged, she could collect irrefutable evidence and execute an arrest of terrorist members bringing them back to the city.

Despite initial resistance from politicians and ethicists, I deployed Toria on a high-risk mission. Within weeks, entire terror clans began being apprehended and brought to justice. Toria had become their worst nightmare, a force they couldn't escape.

My glass drained, I refill it turning on the television to watch the nightly news. I have many meetings ahead of me with politicians, diplomats and ethicists over the next few months, meaning I need to prepare my pitch to employ a team of top scientists to help me build more TRAI robots. I'm exhausted just thinking about this huge task. But, if we are to eradicate terrorists, then it is my duty to do so. I reach for my laptop and begin.

I ARRIVE AT THE LABORATORY, my small team claps as I enter. Toria's achievement has already reached them. Good news travels fast.

"Congratulations Professor." This from my assistant, a woman whose efforts I could not have done without. Elina has the abilities of one twice her age. I'm glad I took a chance with her, she has invaluable skills and will be part of my elite team.

The other four continue clapping.

"Thank you. I see you have already heard that because of Toria and her efforts, we are backed by Madame Secretary and her government along with the Americans and Thames City. I have the authority to employ another thirty scientists so we can keep building TRAI. More will be employed in America and England. We will be required to teach them our methods."

"We're going to need more space."

"That is all part of the plan, Elina. The TRAI Assembly Theatre is being designed as we speak. It will be built in the city centre near The Dungeon. Things will change quickly around here as we need to add more robots as soon as possible. Toria will have her own team and the terrorists won't know what hit them. Now, let's get to work as there is still much to do."

Over many years, I travel teaching more scientists how to build TRAI. I am welcomed in Thames City, New Roma and Hudson State, America. Cities once known as London, Rome and New York.

My small team occasionally accompany me, but mostly I am on my own. I prefer being the only one to teach my skills because then I know things will be done right. The TRAI community will grow and begin to protect the world from terrorists who are trying to take us back to the dystopian war years.

# NINE

Mannix
3038
The Enchanted

MY BODY IS ELECTRIFIED, I'm stoked. Pacing my apartment, I want to tell someone. Toria is the obvious choice and I will let her in on my secret soon, but I need to tweak a few things before I reveal any of this to others. What I also need is someone to practise with, but who?

Researching my powers online I find there are others in the world like me, but they are laying low not wanting to be targeted. I even find out what happened to The Enchanted during the 20-year war. Ninety percent of them were killed. The Enchanted, after years of living at peace with non-magical humans, humans who accepted them, had their community decimated because terrorists saw them as threats, the magic of the Enchanters was strong against the clans. When the wars ended just before the year 3000, skirmishes remained and are still with us today. The Enchanted Community has remained hidden.

I now have my own community of The Enchanted online. We chat regularly, and even though I am safe now, many others still live in fear. Something has to change, non-magical humans and The Enchanted should be living in peace again. This will be my mission.

"You want me to come to your apartment? Is it safe?"

I'm speaking with another Enchanted human, Amber, and trying to convince her to come over and practise with me. "Yes, it is, I promise. It's so cool you live in Harbour City, we can meet in person." Amber hesitates, I can hear her breathe with caution. "Come on, I found you and the others, we're all part of The Enchanted community, this meeting is meant to be.

"Mannix, I don't know you. Online and real life are two very different things."

I sense she's slipping away, I have to do something. "I'll come to you, would that be better? We can meet in a public space if you're more comfortable with that." Again, another pause.

"Maybe that could work. Where? The Town Centre"

I breathe a sigh of relief. "Sure, how about the library? Or the café near it?" I'm rapt when she agrees to meet me at the library.

The library is housed in a building similar to the Dungeon, all of the important buildings in Harbour City were built to withstand terrorist attacks. Can the buildings withstand an attack? This remains to be seen as no terrorist clan has managed to breach the city walls yet.

. . .

I'VE BEEN WAITING fifteen minutes when my transcoder pings.

Running late, be there soon.

I fidget as I wait. Nerves on high alert. I calm myself with thoughts of how Amber and the others can help restore peace between The Enchanted community and non-magical humans, and defeating the terrorist clans will go far in making this happen.

"Sorry. Hi, nice to meet you in person, Mannix." She is puffing, her breathing erratic. I'm stunned, this girl is not a girl, more a woman with a purpose. I think she is close to my age but she looks older, more mature.

"Hi, Amber, likewise. You ok?"

"Um, let's go inside." I follow her into the library, she heads towards the back, but there are not many people around, so I find this unnecessary. But then, I don't know what has happened.

As she leans against the back wall, she explains. "I think I was followed. Only a handful of people know I'm an Enchanted, but I'm pretty sure who it was following me."

Now I know why she didn't want to come to my apartment. It wasn't that she is scared of me, she didn't want to reveal where I live to whoever is following her. "How long have you felt unsafe like this? Harbour City is one of the safest cities in the world."

"Probably my ex, he's unhinged and didn't like that I broke off our engagement." Her breathing has calmed but she is still on edge. Her eyes dart, her hands clenched. With her knees locked and fingers twisting so tight they're turning white, I feel her fear.

Engagement? I want to know more but I don't ask. "Is it ok if I touch your arm, I want you to feel safe with me." I'm assuming having an ex-boyfriend has made her suspicious of everyone. She nods and I place my hand on her arm just below her shoulder giving her a slight squeeze. She sighs, visibly relaxing, and I begin to relax as well.

There are tables near us and I suggest we go and sit, she has said no to going to the café. Too exposed.

She sits, her hands still in a tight ball in her lap. "We're safe here, I want to talk, that's all." She looks at me wide-eyed and nods.

After I tell her what my plans are and what I need from her, I ask her to tell me more about herself.

"I live with my mother and father in the Barracks area. Do you know of those?"

I do. The Barracks were small homes used during the war years by soldiers' families, they are historical and protected. Anyone who lives there requires a lot of paperwork to do renovations and there is no knocking down and rebuilding. I've only been there once, the houses are basically boxes of steel with small windows, each with a small front garden only big enough to hold a few pot plants. This area was once open to terrorist attacks, but now it is gated, so unless you live there, you cannot enter freely, you require an invitation.

"Ok, so you know it is a safe area and it is the only place where I do feel safe. That's why I was scared to meet with you. My brother, Jonathan, has special needs and he keeps my parents busy. He can talk but needs help with everything else. We were lucky to be given a Barracks home because Jon needs special care. My parents pay rent to the government. I count us lucky."

"Do your parents have powers?"

"My father does, like me, he can stun people and turn them to stone if needed. But we both keep a low profile."

She also tells me her mother knows of their powers.

"She is happy we haven't needed to use them for years. I study my craft online wanting to keep the powers in case I need them."

"Of course, yes. So do I. Having only found out I have powers a few months ago, I want to perfect them, which is why I contacted you."

She looks at me curiously, "Why me? There are other people with powers."

"You seem to be the closest and if we're going to practise together, it makes sense to see each other in person."

"So tell me your story. Were you born in Harbour City?"

"No, I was rescued from The Second Zone by Toria and Travis, two TRAI robots. My family was murdered by the terrorists. I was stealing ammunition from them, I wanted revenge. I was surviving on whatever food scraps I could find."

Placing her hand on my arm, she says, "I'm sorry to hear you lost your family, how awful."

"Thanks. It wasn't easy but that anger has fuelled my desire to avenge their deaths. The robots found me at the right time."

Amber nods and smiles at me. Something stirs inside me, she is amiable and likeable.

We continue the conversation and I see she has calmed down enough to be enjoying my company. My body reacts to her being calmer giving me a sense of relief and one of wanting to know her better.

An hour later, I walk her to the bus stop and make sure she is safely on her way before I head home. I gained Amber's trust, now I need to have the whole Enchanted community with me too.

# TEN

Toria

Mission Accomplished

IT'S late afternoon and I'm chasing two terrorist teens when Mannix telepathically stops me. I face plant into the muddy residue of last night's storm.

The teens laugh uproariously, pointing their fingers, "Look at the ancient crappy robot, she can't even stay upright. Ooh, we're so scared of you."

I know what I want to do to the two of them but I'm stopped again by Mannix's voice, "Don't encourage them with an answer Toria. Get back to us, there's more trouble here. I need you here to help with this ambush."

Slowly forcing myself up, I answer Mannix. "Copy that." My circuits are clogged with mud, I'm not even sure he received my reply. I trudge back to the entrance of the Second Zone to both of them laughing. I look towards the other TRAI who are keeping mute, they know not to make fun of a superior.

"Apologies, Toria, but ..." His laughter stops him. "You look, ah ..."

"Stop it, Travis. And you too, Mannix. You've seen mud before haven't you?" I'm hurt by their attitude more than annoyed.

"Yep ok." Mannix is still snickering, "Right, we apprehended a whole clan, they're already on their way to the Dungeon. But they alerted more and ..."

"No need to tell me, I sense they're on their way."

"Good, we're ready for them. Now stay with us, don't get any bold ideas you can do this on your own, Toria." Mannix is giving me an order, not something I'm used to from him but I remain silent. Travis nods towards Mannix and points a finger at me.

I guess I've been told.

We wait near our aeromobile, me picking at the drying mud, shaking off as much as I can. Mannix and Travis are in front, casing the area. They're only a metre away and the rest of our TRAI are ahead of them.

My circuits feel flat, that fall has done more damage than I thought, I must take care. I've engaged stealth mode as I stay with our vehicle. I let them know, "I'll stay back."

Mannix gives me a thumbs up. Within seconds a group bursts through the bush. Only a handful. This is a surprise. Have they been alerted that this is an ambush?

They all trip up on the line Travis had rigged up giving Mannix time to deflect any bullets back to them. They fall hard but are only maimed, we want them alive. A few of the TRAI collect them and bring them back to the waiting area.

More arrive. More bullets zing towards us.

The first few terrorists were a decoy, they were sacrificed so we would not be prepared for the bigger onslaught.

The TRAI group is with Travis fighting them back, but

there are more than we anticipated. I run towards them, they need help. I manage to lift my arm and fire a bullet to the leg on one terrorist before I find myself flat on my face. Again! This time a tree root.

Mannix propels himself towards me while firing, rapidly maiming the rest. Then he uses his telekinesis powers to use the line that stopped the first lot to tie them up. He is also able to stun those who attempt to move.

He had told me about his powers but this is the first time I've seen him in action. Mannix is a huge asset to our cause.

After this lot is deployed to the city, Mannix walks towards me. "Are you ok, that's two falls today."

"This has been another long mission. I feel fried. My circuits have taken a beating. This night air feels icy. And thanks, your powers came in handy. You made light of your powers when you told me about them."

"Let's get you in the vehicle, you need rest. When I told you about my secret I had only known of them for a month. Even I am amazed at how much enchantment is in me."

The night is chilling further and we can hear the nocturnal ferals screech in the nearby desert. The look on his face melts me, my circuits compute how much I want to protect this boy who surprises us every day.

I wonder how much I will rely on Mannix and his powers as my bumbling increases. And Travis too. Obviously, I hope not to deteriorate too quickly but my ageing circuits tell me otherwise.

MADAME SECRETARY IS STANDING in front of her desk and asks her assistant to allow us into her office. We file in, me first, then Travis followed by Mannix. She indicates we sit on the lounge, turning away from us fiddling with something on her desk. Then, she slowly turns towards us and speaks in a worried tone.

"I want to be congratulating you, but my concerns about Toria are increasing. Travis and Mannix, you are both to be commended in how you handled a difficult situation, one hundred and fifty-eight terrorists apprehended."

I try to speak but she stops me by placing her hand up, "You can say your piece soon Toria. The media has been informed of this mission being accomplished with a depleted TRAI taskforce along with the three of you. And it is an accomplishment. However, it is now becoming quite dangerous to go on missions in the Second Zone. The rest of the TRAI community will be informed to be ready for missions. My government and I are contemplating retiring you Toria."

I am stunned but not surprised. My mistakes have increased with each mission, my circuits take longer to recover and I hear creaks throughout my frame. "I understand your concerns, Madame Secretary, but with Mannix and his powers, we now have a real asset against the terrorists. It is my duty to protect him, along with Travis of course."

She moves behind her desk and sits in the black leather chair that houses her fit body snuggly. She smiles, "I think it might be the reverse, Mannix is keeping you out of harm's way. Along with Travis. But I appreciate your request and will ensure it is given to my team, you can still be an asset to the TRAI community for now."

"If I may..." Travis clears his throat. "It is my duty to protect Toria. With the help of Mannix the human, Toria is in safe hands."

"Thank you for your input Travis. Mannix, have you

anything to add before you can all go home and relax for the rest of the day?"

Mannix moves forward on the lounge, his hands in steeple pose. "I do, thank you Madame Secretary. Without these two helping me out of that hell hole Second Zone, I would be dead by now. So yes I would like to keep Toria on the team. I am still perfecting my powers, so the extra help will come in useful."

There is silence in the room for a few minutes. Madame Secretary taps on the desk announcing, "I will do my best to convince my government. However, Toria this is a warning, if you place your colleagues in danger again, you will be dismissed and placed in retirement. Please enjoy the rest of your day." She indicates with her hand that we leave.

We head towards the door, I have my head hanging low.

# ELEVEN

## Toria and The Professor

I LOOK around the Professor's quarters. I take in that his apartment is somewhat larger than mine, which given his status, is appropriate. This housing estate was built for the dignitaries of Harbour City and even though it is fortress-like, it is intended to keep them safe not imprisoned.

I sit in the plush armchair while he is reclined in the one next to me. "How are you Professor Nichols? And thank you for agreeing to meet with me," I ask raising my voice a few octaves, his hearing is not what it used to be.

Before he can answer, his live-in maid, a domestic robot, places tea and biscuits on a small table next to him. "Thank you Besse." He turns to me while he adds three sugars and stirs his tea. "I have a few more aches and pains but they are manageable, thanks for asking. Now, what is it you wanted to discuss?"

I sit with my arms resting on the arm of the chair, trying

to be as close as possible to him so he will hear me clearly, then I say, "You know of my performance of late." He nods acknowledging he *can* hear me. "Well, after the last mission …"

He places his hand up, "The one where you tripped twice?"

"Yes, that's the one. We apprehended one hundred and fifty-eight terrorists despite my issues and the press were complimentary of the result. However, Madame Secretary has mentioned that there are murmurs from her government they want me retired." My head drops. If I was human, my face would be as red as a beetroot right now. This man gave me abilities allowing me to apprehend thousands of terrorists and now I'm embarrassed about what I have become. An old robot placing my team at risk.

He asks me to raise my head and listen to him. He tells me of his feelings when he first designed me and the other TRAIs, how the world is a better place for having the TRAI community to look after them. "I travelled to many places in those dark days teaching other scientists about the wonders of what a TRAI like you could do. They were in awe of such technology and your missions, their missions, have been successful in bringing terrorists to justice. You should be proud of yours and your team's achievements."

He stops momentarily and sips his tea, then speak proudly, "Toria, you and I are both old now. Take me for example, I can barely walk. But your circuits can be repaired, you need to give yourself the time to recover then have them looked at and fixed. You have years in you yet."

I wonder whether he realises how depleted the funds are for the TRAI project, he has been retired for almost two years. "I appreciate I am able to be repaired, but my AI circuits need replacing and upgraded, the budget doesn't allow for this."

He sips his tea and chomps on a biscuit, his vest littered with crumbs. "Ah the dang fangled budget. Sorry, I had an idea things were bad, but things are worse now?"

"Yes, Professor, much worse. You were lucky to be able to complete Travis before the more severe budget cuts were implemented. But there is something more pressing I wanted to speak with you about, it's about Mannix."

"Oh, the boy, how is he? I have been told he is part of The Enchanted Community, who I know have been in hiding since the wars."

"Yes, there are many still in hiding. And they will be a powerful force against terrorists. But this is not about the boy's powers, it is about me and how I ... err, um, relate to him." I pause giving him time to brush down his vest and give me his full attention again. "Protecting him is my top priority and I have ... I mean, I care for him. I have developed human feelings of love. Parental love, that is."

The Professor adjusts his posture having slipped down the chair, then gives me a smile, one that fills his face with joy. His eyes sparkle as he speaks, "I have achieved my dream."

"Professor, whatever do you mean?"

"Toria, you are my first creation. In many ways I feel like your parent, so when I was programming you, without the knowledge of others in my team at the time, I added a list of human feelings to your programming, not quite knowing how it would affect you, or take any effect at all."

"But why Mannix? I protect other humans without such feelings."

Placing his hand on his chin, he thinks for a minute

before answering. "I wish I could tell you, but I have no idea. Emotions are not an exact science. Have you mentioned this to anyone else?"

"No." My tone is adamant. "Only you. And you are the only one I want to know about this. The other TRAI robots may see this as a weakness."

"Or they may want to have the same? Look, Toria, I don't see this as a negative. Use it to your advantage and gain even more of Mannix's trust, learn how he reacts, what influences his enchantments. By keeping your mind on him, your errors may reduce and you will be an asset, not a hindrance."

He may be old but he is just as wise as he has always been. My circuits buzz as I realise his simple solution to my problem may just work. I'm about to say thanks when I see the professor has fallen asleep. It's time I leave.

Besse closes the door behind me. She is even older than I am, but being a domestic robot, her ageing circuits don't require the upkeep mine do.

NOISES STOP me in my tracks. Turning back towards the professor's estate, I run. I had walked only a few metres. My sensors are scrambled with fear, on high alert.

Besse is at the security gate with two people I don't recognise. They are dressed in weathered black clothing, their hoods on. This area is a high-priority safe zone, the only people allowed are the dignitaries who live here, their staff and their handful of visitors like me.

I detect that Besse is distressed. The two people I can now identify - one male, one female. They take off running as they notice me. I reach Besse but she turns towards the Professor's entrance and enters without acknowledging me. Strange? Why didn't she talk to me? But there is no time, I need to catch the two humans, something tells me there is a problem and they have taken part in it.

Telepathically messaging Travis, I use my sensors to find the runaways, who I suspect are terrorists. But how? No terrorist has ever stepped foot in the city since the wars.

Travis answers via transcoder, "Message received. On route to the east side of the estate. Have alerted Mannix."

This is good, I will have back up soon. Giving my optical sensors a boost, I scan the area. It is deathly quiet with any children at school and adults at work by now. I detect sound and the two are heading east. Perfect, Travis should be there by the time they arrive. An electric fence guards that side with double wire on top. If they came in this way, how did they bypass the electricity?

The transcoder crackles, "I have sight. There are two in black clothing?"

"Yes, be careful Travis, I suspect they are terrorists. They will be armed and possibly have a bomb or have placed a bomb in the complex." I don't know that they have done such a thing, but I call for more reinforcements to scour the site in case my instincts are correct. Then I hear shots. "Travis. Travis, what's happening?"

"There has been gunfire. I'm safe."

I hear voices, maybe reinforcements have arrived. "I'm on my way, brief the reinforcements. This breach in our security is serious."

I arrive to chaos. More terrorists and rebel TRAI have breached the city's security boundary. I reach Travis and Mannix to find them struggling to keep them at bay. "Mannix, use your enchantments."

"I have, Toria. I have stunned many of them, but they

are streaming in from other parts. Where are the reinforcements?"

My body shakes with the fear of what may happen. This is a new sensation. "I thought they were already here. They must be on their way." I say this to reassure me more than anything. But what has taken so long? My sensors go into overdrive.

# TWELVE

Mannix

Enchantments and Reinforcements

THE FENCE WAS TAMPERED with in several places, this is where the terrorists are entering. I'm using my enchantments, all of them, but there are too many terrorists charging towards me. I concentrate on disarming the rebel TRAI. Where are those reinforcements?

"Travis, send another message, we can't do this on our own."

Travis is fending off as many terrorists as he can. Explosions rupture the air, the citizens are in danger. I see him send another message and he hands the transcoder to me, "Madame Secretary is on the line."

I listen to her for a few minutes as she says, "I have been given news of the Professor." She tells me the news and I know I have to tell Toria, she will be devastated. The shock hits me hard, I can only imagine how Toria will feel.

Madame Secretary continues, "This attack is a disaster,

Mannix. I have sent reinforcements, they are already in the north and west. More are on their way to you. Please stop this situation from escalating." Thanking Madame Secretary, I hand the transcoder back to Travis who is still fending off terrorists along with a few other TRAIs I see have arrived. But we need more.

Forgetting the bad news for now, I focus on using one of my enchantments to throw more ammunition towards terrorists when I notice the other TRAI robots, most of our team, in the distance. They are battling the terrorists from that end.

Toria heads towards us. "Finally reinforcements. Have them secure the fences Travis and leave some guards there to keep watch for more entering."

At least 50-strong terrorists are heading towards us. They are armed with shotguns and grenades. Explosions are blasting as a grenade is flung at us. I use my deflecting powers and send the grenade back to the terrorists. Some are maimed. Our TRAI scramble towards them placing them under guard.

Suddenly flames leap out towards the terrorists, Travis has used his incineration power. The area we are in is hushed momentarily after screams had lashed at us. My feelings are jumbled with fear and uncertainty. We need to get this scum out of the city. I take this lull in fighting to address Travis.

"Head back towards the Professor's house and use more of your incineration power. Join in with the reinforcements. Toria and I will head to the northern area. We need to stop this catastrophe."

"Affirmative," yells Travis as he runs off.

We hear from the TRAI who secured the northern area

that no citizens were hurt, lucky most of them were at school or work.

With the reprieve in the fighting still with us, I turn to Toria. "I have some bad news."

AS TRAVIS and the others secure the maimed terrorists and rebel TRAI, Toria and I head to the Professor's house. When we arrive it is quiet, very quiet.

There is no one here. We assume Besse has been taken to The Dungeon for questioning. I guess we will find out soon enough what her fate will be.

Toria is sitting on a lounge chair staring into space, I am standing behind the lounge. She had not said a word until now.

"I was sitting with him, right here. Right in this chair." Her words are choked with guilt and despair. "Those terrorists will pay for this, the Professor's murder will not be in vain." Her head is slumped. I place my hand on her shoulder not knowing what to say but letting her know I'm listening. "Mannix, he was a father-figure to me. An extraordinary human. How do I go on without him?"

I'm puzzled at her admission about the Professor. It's a strange thing for a robot to say, it is rather emotional. "Toria, what do you mean?

"Wha ... oh, having known the Professor for so long, who will replace him? That's what I meant. I was his first TRAI, we had a connection."

I understand the connection thing, but she had used the term, 'father-figure', that is so un-robot-like. I think she is experiencing human feelings but I let it go for now. I do like the idea she is human-like in her thoughts, it makes me feel closer to her. But for now she seems distraught, if this is possible for a robot. I decide not to make things worse for her, this is something we can discuss another time if needed.

I come around and sit on the lounge as we continue to talk about how we managed to bring the terrorists down, many were killed, the ones who survived are now at The Dungeon. The fence will be reinforced and TRAI guards will be deployed throughout the city. Madame Secretary does not want a repeat of this. We are thankful no citizens were hurt other than... The Professor. Sadness envelops me. He being a dignitary will mean there will be an investigation, how did the terrorists get to Besse?

"The Professor will be honoured with a state funeral, his legacy is large, people will not forget him," I tell Toria. Madame Secretary had sent me this message while we were walking to the house in silence. She asked how Toria was doing and I let her know she was not in a great spot.

"That is the least we can do for him. I will not let people forget him, Mannix. He deserves a statue too, this is something I will discuss with his team and we can take a proposal to Madame Secretary." Her voice is strangely calm now, the emotion has left her, she is now focusing on the Professor's legacy.

I bow my head then sigh. "Toria, there is time to think of things like that, let's have him buried first. But I understand your desire to honour him." She looks at me, if she was human she would be sobbing, so I decide to change the subject.

"May I talk to you about someone I met recently?" When she nods without focus, I continue talking but know she is still thinking of her loss. "I met with another member of The Enchanted community, she lives at The Barracks. Her name is Amber and we have been training together. There are also more of the Enchanters around the world, all lying low since the wars. We now have an online group and discuss our powers."

Toria's arm is bent, her head in her hand as she listens. She raises her head and looks up. I think her eyes a little brighter but know this isn't possible for a robot. "Oh, I'm happy there are more of your kind, this is excellent."

"It is my mission, apart from fighting the terrorists, to bring The Enchanted community back into the mainstream, we don't deserve to be hidden. We may need your help and we can be useful in helping to remove the terrorist scourge once and for all."

She stands with her arms outstretched. I stand as well. Placing her arms around me she says, "That is an honourable mission, one I will help you with as much as needed."

She hugs me for an uncomfortable amount of time not realising she is squeezing the breath out of me.

# THIRTEEN

Toria

The Professor's Legacy

HUNDREDS OF TRAI robots stand guard as the coffin passes. They bow their heads for the Professor. And for me as I lead the procession. How I managed to pull myself together to be here today required all of my strength. If this is grief, then I feel sorry for humans. The hurt has weakened me, hit me to the core of my circuits, I still don't know how I'm going forward from this.

The Professor's team, Madame Secretary, dignitaries from the scientific community and overseas dignitaries from Thames City, New Roma and Hudson City, all march behind me and the coffin. Many thousands of people line the harbour foreshore braving the drizzling rain.

This is being broadcast the world over, such was his presence. I have controlled my feelings to the point I feel more robotic than ever. A part of me has died with him, I know I will never recover but am determined for the Professor's legacy to be remembered and to make the terrorists pay.

Arriving at the funeral boat, the coffin is placed on it. His wishes to be cremated on the harbour are being adhered to. The boat is moored in a spot where there was once a pylon of the Sydney Harbour Bridge, if it still existed. Much of Sydney's landmarks were destroyed during the wars, as were many other icons around the world. So many of the human designed and built iconic achievements are now only memories or regaled to the history books.

Prior to the funeral, I had discussed with the professor's team and Madame Secretary my desire to erect a statue in front of the TRAI Assembly Theatre. Discussions are still going ahead with the Board. I will not rest until this happens.

Mannix and Travis stand next to me as we watch the funeral people prepare the boat. I feel my legs weaken as the torch is thrown onto the deck near the coffin. Mannix and Travis hold me up. Grief has taken hold, my joints weakened, my head swimming with images of him, Professor Hugh Nichols, the man I am proud to call my father.

"WHAT DO you mean there are no funds left?" I am in Madame Secretary's office. She is seated in her glory in the overlarge executive chair and is wearing comfortable activewear giving her a more relaxed air.

"I didn't say that Toria, I said, 'funds are limited' and we are still in discussions. I loosen up as she continues, "We only had the funeral a few weeks ago, give us some time to organise things. Do you have an artist in mind?"

"No, but I will be happy to research this. I want the best, his statue has to be his exact likeness."

"As you wish. Now, I was about to go for a run. Is there anything else?"

"Yes, what will happen to Besse, the Professor's domestic robot?"

"She will receive a fair trial, however, aiding and abetting terrorists is a criminal offence. Whether she knew they were planning to enter the city, we are yet to find out. But she is an accomplice in the professor's death, she will be jailed until her circuits fail, she won't be bothering you again I assure you."

Poor old Besse, who knows what they promised her. Or threatened her with. I detected anxiety coming from her that day. The trial will tell us all what happened, I feel sad that a robot has been manipulated in this way, no different to the rebel TRAIs, the terrorists had learned how to do this is and it is something we must be more mindful of.

I stand and head towards the door, "Thank you for your time on a Sunday, Madame Secretary. I appreciate it. Enjoy your run."

As I walk out of her office the building is deserted as would be the case on a Sunday. I hadn't heard from Madame Secretary since the funeral and was keen to speak with her before my request was forgotten, so she had agreed to meet with me this morning. I know we have little funds to work with but I don't want this pushed aside for some other insignificant cause.

I'm heading home when I receive a message from Mannix asking if I'm home. I message back saying I'll be home in ten minutes.

. . .

MANNIX IS at my door with someone I assume is Amber. He introduces us.

"Hi, both of you. Nice to meet you, Amber. Please, come in."

Mannix makes himself at home on the lounge, as always. He indicates to Amber to sit next to him. She seems shy and is a lithe little human, she looks like she scares easily. I detect anxiety. But I also detect a strong young woman when she needs to be, she has a purpose. Where Mannix is dark and classically handsome with still some maturing to happen, Amber is already mature with blonde locks and bright blue eyes. Mannix will tower over her once he completes his growth spurts.

"I wanted to talk to you about our ideas to help The Enchanted community integrate into society again and with the help of the TRAI community, we think we can make it happen."

"Ok, Mannix, I'm here to listen. May I offer you some refreshments? Drink?"

"Err, no thank you." This from Amber. And it's almost a whisper.

"Na, I'm good, thanks," says Mannix who I sense is keen to talk.

He rattles off what their plan is at such a speed I have to ask questions to slow him down. "Look, I know you're excited about this but speak slower. My older brain takes longer to process things now." This combined with the added grief still swarming my body has slowed my circuits.

"Oh, yes. Sorry, Toria."

He continues telling me of the team he has assembled online. This includes Amber and two other young males from the two regional areas down the south coast. Amber has the power to turn offenders temporarily to stone, the two males have the power of flight – they can propel themselves in any direction.

Mannix shows me photos of the two males. One is slight and lanky, his height will be an asset. The other is stocky, his muscles ripped with veins about to pop.

"You have done well, these two will be strong assets for us. But only two?"

"The Enchanters are still wary of coming out, we may entice a few more once the two boys are with us, but it hasn't been easy convincing them."

"That's understandable but a few more will be beneficial to your cause." I turn towards Amber, "And along with you Amber, I am sure we can put a good dent into the terrorist population."

I then turn my attention back to Mannix. "Have you organised the two males to come to the city? We need you all trained up to face the terrorists."

Mannix looks at Amber then turns to me, "Amber has been training with me, we have been practising our enchantments, but yes, she and the other two definitely need some combat training. The boys will be arriving next week by train."

"That's great, you are organised. I will advise Travis and we will find times to suit all of you. Mannix you can help with this training."

He nods and they both stand to leave. "Toria, you're the best, I knew I could count on you," he says as he opens the door allowing Amber out. She waves goodbye.

Oh my heart, if I had one. would be carrying the quiet caring I have for this human I saved.

# FOURTEEN

Mannix

The Team is Ready

WE ARE ASSEMBLED in the common room, a few TRAI who have helped me to train the two Enchanters who volunteered to join us. I have now accepted that these are the only people willing to risk their lives and to out themselves as Enchanters, but I am disappointed we didn't attract more recruits.

Six weeks training will have to do too. My team is strong with enchantment powers, the training they have received just enhances what they already have. And Toria, who was hesitant at first due to missing the Professor, now agrees we have to again seek out the terrorists before they can regroup and attack the city again.

"Everyone be ready tomorrow morning at 06:00. I have transport organised and many of the TRAI community has been deployed to The Second Zone today. The two hundred left here will travel with us tomorrow. And a word of warning to our new recruits, don't try to be heroes, we work as a team."

"Yes, Toria." Amber and the two boys answer in unison.

As we disperse, I take Toria aside. "May I speak with you?"

She takes a bottle of oil and begins the process of oiling her ageing body, wanting to be fully prepared for this mission. She wants us to severely maim the terrorist enclaves, bring them down as vengeance for the slaying of the Professor. "Sure, speak away."

"Amber. I ... umm, I want to be sure she is protected. I don't want to lose her."

Placing her hands on my arms, I sense her caring nature, something that warms my heart, she is a sort of mother figure to me, which I find comforting. She speaks with faint concern, "Mannix, it's obvious you two young people are close and we will do our best to minimise casualties from our team. Now, go and get some rest, we all need to be a full strength tomorrow."

AMBER HAD AGREED to stay with me at my apartment because of the early start. Her face is full of concern, her voice quiet, almost shy. "I umm, I'm not sure ..." she clears her throat, "Mannix, we are taking a huge risk, even if we defeat the terrorists who is to say we in The Enchanted community will be accepted again?"

Unfortunately, she is right to be concerned. I sit on the lounge with her and say with a calmness I don't feel, "We are a strong team and the TRAI are trained for these types of missions. Our powers enhance their forces and we will make the world see that Enchanters have a purpose and deserve to be part of society once more. There is no need for us to hide any longer."

Her eyes glisten with tears, which she stops from falling with a sigh full of what I think indicates she is hopeful. Placing her hands on my face, she kisses my forehead, then my cheeks. Her eyes meet mine and I kiss her full lips, something I've been aching to do since we met.

She places her head on my chest, "I trust your judgement, Mannix."

I lift her head and kiss her deeply, with passion this time. She returns my feelings, something that pleases me. Looking deep into my eyes, she smiles placing her head on my chest again. My arms are around her as I focus on what she has said, it lifts the shallow darkness I have been feeling, maybe together we can help to eradicate the terrorists. With peace around us then we can concentrate of bringing The Enchanted into the open once more.

WE ARE STAKED out in the Second Zone. TRAIs are closest to the enclaves, we Enchanters, Toria and Travis are with the vehicles in an area with a view of the enclaves. We're ready to head into the attack zone when needed.

"It's unusually quiet," whispers Toria in the subdued morning light, "no animal noises, no human noises either."

"The terrorists have been in hiding since their attack on the city." This from Travis as he scans the area. "We need to be on the lookout for rebel TRAI as well, who knows what the terrorists have programmed them to do to us.

"Oh yes, the robots who were captured and were turned against us. They are probably programmed to target other TRAI," adds Toria

With Amber by my side whose fear is tangible, what I'm

about to say is more for her benefit than for anyone else, "We have the forces to combat the terrorists and their rebels, Toria, but don't be too fooled, we know they can be devious." Then, almost on cue, we hear our TRAI forces march towards the terrorists' homes with me hoping the women and children have been taken to safety. I remember the fear gripping me when my family was slaughtered. And this is the motivation I need to eradicate this evil, I want the world to be a better place without the terrorist scourge taunting us.

From our vantage point and through the cicadas incessant call, we hear gunfire, metal creaking, screams, and see explosions from every corner. The feral animals have been awakened too. Some snakes slither past us along with huge kangaroos, some two headed ones with joeys, escaping further into the outback to relative safety. This bushland might give animals shelter and food, but guns, smoke and being trampled alive, send them scurrying.

Toria and Travis deploy. "Follow us, stay close. Use your enchantments as needed but don't put yourselves in danger."

As we near the battleground, the bush surrounding the terrorists' enclave is embroiled with smoke, turning the morning sun into a dim grey smear. Over a hundred TRAI have surged forward, their movements sharp and exact, marching with purpose. Blades slide from their arms, gun barrels snap from their shoulders, and their eyes lock onto the father figures standing defiant protecting their clans.

Toria darts ahead with twin steel knives flashing from her wrists. Sparks scatter as she collides midair with terrorists leaping towards her. Beside her, Travis spreads his arms wide, his incineration powers inflict fire onto the terrorists targeting him. They fall like dominoes with ear-piercing screams emitted from their charred bodies.

Amber and I are using our enchantments as best we can, but they keep coming. The boys are behind us, scouting if terrorists are going to take us from behind in this part of the bush. They obviously find some because we hear the boys shooting occasionally, but our focus is on what is happening in front of us. Terrorists are finding their way through the thick bush and many stare us down before shooting. This is their domain and they know how to use it. We duck and weave as best we can, Amber always staying close to me.

We're still behind Toria and Travis when I realise the two Enchanters, the boys ... I can no longer hear them. Calling out, there is no response. "We need to find them. Can you see them, Amber?"

"No, they were behind us and now they're not there." Her voice cracks with emotion and fear.

After advising Toria what is happening, I indicate to Amber to 'follow me'. We head back the way we came. We scour the area and it is only minutes when we find them, both lying still on the harsh bush soil. They have been shot dead. Amber lets out a gasp.

"There must be snipers, we need to get back to the protection of the TRAIs. Stay close."

"Why didn't we hear the snipers? The boys were right behind us. We can't just leave them here, Mannix."

"Snipers have silencers on their weapons. I just alerted the medics, there's not much more we can do. Come on, we have to move or we'll end up like them." I know I sound cruel and place my hand on her arm, giving her a reassuring squeeze, "We can't do anything for them now, please Amber, we need to finish this mission."

We find the TRAIs, with Toria and Travis having integrated with the main group now. Along the way Amber found her strength and stunned a few terrorists and I was able to deflect their ammunition back to them.

The battle continues with casualties on both sides. I'm thinking of the two Enchanters we lost when Toria calls my name. We head towards her and Travis.

"We have the upper hand, they will surrender soon. Travis will take the rebel TRAI and have them transported back to the city. We were able to capture twelve of them, Mannix."

"Great, just in time too. Our casualties are many. We lost the two boys, the Enchanters. Amber and I found their bodies back there." I indicate towards where we came from, "we need to finish this once and for all."

# FIFTEEN

Toria

Retirement is on Hold

I SIT with nervous anticipation in the television studio. The harsh studio lights shine bright on my metallic body. I'm about to be interviewed by a reporter for a story on a news special. The audience had clapped and cheered when I walked on set making me feel the best I've felt since losing the Professor. I feel lighter, the sadness placed in a part of my circuits only to be visited when I'm alone and want to be with him.

After this latest mission, we came back to a hero's welcome with Madame Secretary showering us with praise even though we lost almost half of the TRAI community. This loss hits me almost as hard as the loss of the Professor, these were my colleagues, they will be missed. But we managed to end the terrorist threat with the capture of the two heads of the biggest clans along with several hundreds of their followers. The few who are left are mainly elderly women, mothers and young children, they shouldn't cause us any trouble. They had come out of hiding after we transported their leaders. The twelve TRAI rebel robots will be decommissioned if they are not salvageable. If some can be reprogrammed they will be added to our depleted TRAI community.

Travis and Mannix were also asked to be part of this interview but they declined saying I was the best one to talk about the mission, how we avenged the Professor, and ensuring the citizens of Harbour City understand we are doing our best to keep them safe. In Mannix's case, he is not ready to speak about The Enchanted community just yet. I had disagreed with him and had wanted him to celebrate what he and Amber, and the two boys we lost, had done to help us. Mannix shut me down saying he will discuss this when he and Amber are ready. Deciding to allow this for them, I agreed on doing the interview solo.

The reporter steps on set and once we're miked up, she starts.

"You will know my guest tonight, she has been an integral part of the TRAI team eradicating the terrorists from the Second Zone. With the loss of Professor Hugh Nichols still on her mind, I'd like to introduce Toria, a robot we very much needed ... and still need. Welcome Toria."

"Thank you for having me. I appreciate your kind words."

"This last mission, tell us about what happened?"

"The terrorists have increased their missions against us over the past few years, they want control of Harbour City. The targeted attack on our city where we lost the esteemed Professor Hugh Nichols... I was his first build as you know, spurred us on to organise this mission and try to end the terrorist scourge before they somehow managed to take control of our city."

"I am sorry for your loss, Toria, it is well-known you were the Professor's first TRAI. And the terrorists breaking into our city was frightening for all of us. We are grateful for what you and your team has done, will this mean peace?"

"I truly hope so. We managed to secure heads of clans and many of their followers along with the rebel TRAI, there were only a dozen or so of them. However, we remain vigilant as there is no way of knowing if some terrorist leaders are left and are now in hiding. We are relatively safe for now. The Second Zone will be monitored day and night. My TRAI team will alert us of any further threats."

"That is reassuring for all of us here in Harbour City. So, where to from here? What does Toria do next?"

I pause for effect and turn to the audience, "I was built to protect and serve humans and this is my main focus, always will be. The Professor's legacy lives within me and every TRAI robot. I will continue to do my duty for however long I have." The audience erupts with cheers and more clapping.

The interview continues with the reporter asking relevant questions of me so as to inform his audience their security is our top priority. His final question has the audience erupting with cheers and giving me a standing ovation.

"Toria, do you feel you and your team have done enough?"

"Yes, yes I do." I turn towards the audience, addressing them again, "we understand how fearful you are of the terrorists, and more so now that they entered our city. But let me reassure you and all citizens of Harbour City, your TRAI will do everything in their power to stop the terrorists. Our mission is and always will be to keep our city safe.

This is no different to all of the TRAI community scattered throughout what is left of our world. We work as teams to protect all citizens."

The reporter allows the audience to settle before speaking again. "Well, on behalf of everyone here and the citizens of Harbour City, I thank you for your service, Toria, and hope the terrorist threat has truly ended. Please thank Toria everyone."

As the audience cheer me on, I shake the reporter's hand and step off the set once the microphone is removed.

It's still early morning, so after the interview I am driven back to the common room of the Assembly Theatre. This is where I find everyone.

"How did it go?" Mannix is the first to speak after I walk in.

"Good, I think. The audience was responsive and the reporter seemed pleased. Watch it tonight and make your own judgement."

"Will do. Now, we've organised a surprise for you with the help of Madame Secretary and her government."

He turns to pick up a small, bright blue velvet box and walks towards me. Amber, Travis and other TRAI are watching on, some relaxed, others I detect have some excited anticipation.

His voice is warm and loving, "Toria, I am more than grateful for you rescuing me, I would not be living today if not for you. And Travis, of course." He turns to Travis who bows reverently. "Your body has taken damage most other TRAI would not be able to endure, but you refuse to give up. These are for you."

He hands me the box and I rub my hand over its velvety softness. Unlatching the gold clasp, I open it. My eyes don't register the vials at first, or the crystalline blue of the liquid contained within. There are three nestled in the rich golden silk fabric. "Are these what I think they are?"

"I don't know, are they?"

"Mannix, stop it, you know exactly what they are. Liquid gold. These processors will restore my circuits, reinforce my core frame."

"They're blue actually," he laughs, "but yes this is exactly what they will do. And also heal those nasty microfractures you have been neglecting."

For a long moment, I remain still, my feelings deepen as I admire Mannix and my team. "I ... wow. I wasn't expecting this." My voice is quiet and mechanical in its uniformity. "Thank you."

Mannix moves towards me enveloping me in a hug. "Consider this gift a boost to the Professor's legacy, giving it more prestige. It's a promise. You stay with us. For as long as you want."

I straighten with pride hearing this. "My, this is wonderful. I'll make sure these are put to good use."

"And there's more," says Mannix as he cues the music. "It's time we let our hair down and partied."

My circuits buzz with gratitude. This boy has my circuits as if they were my heart and soul. How I wish I had those. He knows how much I care about him and how I want to protect him for as long as possible. I know it was his idea to approach Madame Secretary in securing this box, the greatest gift he could have given this old robot.

# SIXTEEN

Toria
The Statue

AFTER SPENDING six relentless months searching for the perfect artist to sculpt the Professor's statue, scouring the remnants of a fractured world for someone worthy of the task, I found someone suitable, a master sculptor who hails from Italy. I found his ethereally beautiful body of works that now stand in the battered but resilient Vatican Square, one of the few fragments of Vatican City to endure the ravages of the wars, but only just. Restoration crews still labour day and night, breathing life back into what was once a beacon of the Catholic Church. St. Peter's Cathedral has been under careful restoration since the Professor built me, so it seems natural that this sculptor be the one to create the statue.

Although many citizens of our world are atheists, there are many believers still within Vatican City who want Catholicism to have a resurgence. It is these people who are helping fund restorations and lobbying governments to keep their dream alive. They also lobbied not to change the name of the city, wanting it to be a beacon of hope for future generations.

Three Italian cities survived the wars – Rome now known as New Roma, Milan now Central City and Florence now Lumina, the city of light. However, they are still all in various states of repair. This is the case for many cities around the world. In Harbour City we lost icons like the Sydney Harbour Bridge and the Sydney Opera House, but we were fortunate to be isolated from the European cities and their devastation because they were at the centre of the wars. America was also fortunate but like Australia, fewer than 20 regions remain there.

ANTONIO LIPARO, the sculptor, is arriving this morning and I, along with Madame Secretary, am waiting for him to come through customs. Although Madame Secretary is quiet, I sense she is excited to meet this artisan and is now fully onboard with this project, one close to my heart, albeit a mechanical one.

We wait. And we wait. I keep scanning the airport in case he enters from another door. Although this is unlikely, I spin my head around often, seeking him out. It seems everyone has come out of the arrival doors, no one has come through the doors for at least an hour. "What if something has happened to him?"

"Let me check, wait here." I watch on with nervous twitches as Madame Secretary talks into her transcoder walking towards the security entrance and disappears into customs.

My patience is wearing thin when finally the doors

open and Madame Secretary is beside Antonio, both smiling. Well, that's a good sign.

As we drive Antonio to his hotel, he explains why he was the last passenger out. We listen to his thick Italian accent, "My apologies, but your customs officers are thorough. They checked all of my luggage because I had placed a box of sample paints, non-flammable, in my second bag. An oversight on my part. They were being overly cautious. I can't say I blame them considering the world we live in now."

"We understand, Antonio, there is no harm done. You will be able to rest at your hotel, we have a meeting at my office at 10am tomorrow. Please enjoy your rest and Toria and I will see you then."

After stepping out of the car in front of the hotel, Antonio nods as he shakes her hand and bows his head towards me.

THE FIVE OF US, Mannix, Travis, Madame Secretary, Antonio and me are standing out the front of Assembly Theatre, which is to be renamed as 'The Nichols Centre', another one of my ideas to honour the Professor's legacy.

"A plinth will be erected here, this is where the statue will stand."

"That is good," says Antonio, his thick Italian accent evident again. "I will design the statue to be the Professor's height, 175cm. Will the plinth be big enough to support the weight?"

"Now that we know the statue's height, we will have the plinth made to the right specifications," Madame Secretary informs him.

We continue to speak with Antonio about the finer

details, Travis listens patiently but gives no input. Antonio agrees to show us preliminary drawings in the next two weeks and will begin once these are approved.

"Where is my studio?"

I answer him, "There is a room in the Assembly Theatre you can use. It is soundproof, you will not be disturbed nor will you disturb the scientists and TRAI in the building. Follow me, I will show you all where it is."

In the few months that follow Antonio's arrival, I visit him often in the soundproof room wanting to see his progress. His skills as an artisan are evident as I see the Professor's statue take shape. I am pleased with my choice of artist and hope the Professor agrees with me.

"FELLOW DIGNITARIES, citizens of Harbour City and visitors, I welcome you all to the unveiling of 'The Nichols Centre', the new name of the Assembly Theatre. With this new name comes another unveiling, that of Professor Hugh Nichols' statue as a testament to his work within these hallowed walls." Madame Secretary waits for the clapping and cheers to subside before continuing, "It is my pleasure to introduce you to the artist, Antonio Liparo who hails from the city of New Roma, Italy. Please put your hands together for our creator of what you will soon see is a masterpiece, I'm sure."

Antonio stands next to me bowing and clapping his hands towards Madame Secretary and the dignitaries standing with her, then towards me. I bend slightly towards him in thanks. Once there is silence, Antonio thanks the crowd and tells us how much he has enjoyed his time in our beautiful city. "You are all blessed to be living in paradise." There are a few cheers and claps from the crowd. "There has been more sunshine here than I have ever seen, a sense of safety and calm, and a people who are friendly and accommodating. I am honoured to have been asked to produce a statue of the eminent Professor Hugh Nichols that will be unveiled by his greatest achievement, Toria and your Madame Secretary." He turns towards us indicating we stand with him.

If I could, I would be blushing now. I am the Professor's greatest achievement, but to hear it mentioned by someone who doesn't know me that well is humbling. I keep listening to the rest of Antonio's speech where he praises Madame Secretary and names the others who have helped him with this project. "It is now time for the unveiling. Madame Secretary and Toria, would you please do the honours."

We walk over to the statue that is draped in a deep blue velvet fabric, the Professor's favourite colour, and each take the rope on either side. We pull.

The crowd erupts, cameras flash and news reporters clamber to ask us questions.

I look into the statue's eyes and see my creator, my father. Looking around I whisper, "I hope wherever you are Professor, you are happy with this likeness of you. I know I am."

# SEVENTEEN

Mannix

The Planning Begins

INFORMING the two families of the boys who died while helping us was the hardest thing I've had to do in my young life. They were awarded medals of valour that gave their families some sense of peace.

That was last week and the fathers of the two boys offered to help in any way they are able. I told them I would keep this in mind. Who knows what type of help I will need to convince The Enchanted to come forward and live within the wider community again?

I arrive at The Barracks and am standing at the front door of Amber's home. To say I am nervous is an understatement and it is increasing my fear of being judged. Who am I? I'm a kid from the Second Zone with a desire to avenge my family's murders. Will my anger show, am I good enough for their daughter? Is Amber being three years older than me going to be an issue?

I suck in a deep breath, my mouth dry from the anticipation when Amber opens the door. She looks up and plants a light kiss on my lips. I begin to breathe a little easier. Following her down a small hallway, I walk into a back room housing a galley kitchen, small round dining table and a wheelchair where Jon, Amber's brother, sits staring at this stranger in his home. Jon makes screeching noises piercing my ears.

"Calm down Jon, Mannix is not here to take you away from us," reassures his mother. Jon calms instantly. I watch as she strokes his face while lovingly looking into his eyes. I find out how well she uses her motherly skills as the night progresses.

Lyra greets me warmly once Jon is calm, along with Wilban, Amber's dad and my nervousness takes a step back, I feel at home in their presence. Lyra cannot be mistaken for anyone other than Amber's mother, she is an older version of her. Wilban is a little intimidating with a muscular body and is at least a head taller than me. And I wouldn't call myself short.

"Please, take a seat Mannix, dinner is almost ready." Lyra heads towards the kitchen with Amber.

"Yes, sit. I'd like to get to know you better." Wilban indicates to the chair next to where Jon is seated. I hesitate initially, but when Jon shows no interest, I calm myself and sit.

"Amber tells us you are an Enchanter and want The Enchantment Community to come forward, show ourselves."

"That's correct, Mr Sarkington." I clear my throat. He is seated next to me and I feel overpowered by his size. "There is no reason for us to remain hidden any longer. And, with the two boys sacrificing their lives for our cause, it would be a waste not to at least try."

He nods then asks me about my life, "For one so young, you are ambitious. Tell us more."

As Lyra and Amber place food on the table I give a short rundown of where I come from, how I was rescued and how I began my mission to bring all Enchanters together. "We have a long way to go, but it is achievable now the terrorists have been removed."

"Hmm, let's hope that is the case. I'm sure if any remained they will regroup. But for now, we can bask in this safety. Please eat."

The evening goes fast with Lyra having to appease Jon a few times. His refusal to eat vegetables brought back memories of when I was young, they weren't my favourite things to eat either. Lyra's touch in calming Jon was impressive, something I spoke to Amber about later.

WE ARE ALONE in her room, the small TV giving off a pale light. She has her head on my chest, my hand playing with her hair. "Your mother has a real touch with Jon, she's amazing."

"She says that is her magical power. We're lucky she has it, Jon can be a handful because of his size, which he inherited from Dad. I took after mum's side of the family," she laughs.

"Your father was intimidating at first, but he made me feel welcome. I like your parents."

"They're ok. As parents, I mean." She looks up at me and notices my face. "Oh, I'm sorry, I didn't mean ..."

"It's fine. My parents were ok and I miss them, but it

doesn't mean you shouldn't talk about yours." I move towards her small desk changing the subject, "now, where's your laptop, let's chat with our other Enchanter friends, we need to come up with a plan."

# EIGHTEEN

Toria

Strength comes from Within

I AM with Travis at the home of Amber's family attending a birthday party for Mannix. He had chosen to celebrate it at Amber's home because of the warmth he has felt whenever he is in the family's company. His own apartment had not been an option due to its starkness and lack of size.

"Alright, it's time to cut the cake. Mannix, come stand behind it. And what a lovely cake, it's lovely even if I say so myself." Mannix does as he is told as we all laugh at Mr Sarkington's joke about his baking.

"It looks good enough to eat," laughs Mannix as he listens to us all sing Happy Birthday to him. Even Jon joins in by swaying in his chair and clapping his hands.

My boy has turned twenty-one and my sensors are filled with pride. Even Travis seems to be standing taller.

"Speech. Speech."

"Thank you Mr and Mrs Sarkington for showing me

your love and hospitality these past two years. And now, let's enjoy this masterpiece."

Travis and I watch on as the humans eat. The cake tastes better than it looks according to Mannix and Amber, but Mannix is impressed that her father actually went to the trouble of baking it. This is a day of celebration on two fronts, one is Mannix becoming a man and leaping into adulthood long before his time, the other is that the plan to bring The Enchantment Community back into society, has begun. Mannix and Amber have created support from both sides – the non-magical and the magical - with the help of the TRAI community. There are a growing number of Enchanters wanting to take part and alliances with sympathetic leaders around the world, including Madame Secretary. There have been many secret meetings to bring about unifying humans with The Enchanted Community as they once were. It's a slow process, but progress is happening.

History showed that the terrorists turned public opinion against Enchanters during the war years. They spread rumours of dark magic being used on women and children and how the Enchanters caused havoc when their magic went wrong. This was due to terrorists using AI to generate false images of destruction and mayhem. Terrorists and Enchanters fought many battles, which unfortunately, gave the terrorist enclaves the upper hand.

Now, with terrorists largely captured the world over, this secret plan will come to fruition when The Enchanted Community is ready to stand with all humans again. The next step is to show society the positive side of this community and how together they will make the world a better place.

My pride shows as we chat with Amber's family getting to know them better. This is only the third time I have met her parents even though both Travis and I have been helping with the plan. Today is a social and happy event, one that brings me even closer to Mannix. And now Amber too. It is a pleasure to see Mannix have a family of his own once more.

WE ARE at The Nichols Centre and all assembled in the same room where Antonio Liparo had weaved his magic. Mannix and Amber are on stage, one that was purpose built for these meetings. Travis is seated in the front row with me, Madame Secretary and her team, and a handful of trusted dignitaries. The second row is filled with selected members of the TRAI community. This secret plan is still too fragile to involve too many others. The rest of the chairs are filled with selected Enchanters who have come from all over the world – England, Italy, France, Spain, Greece and the USA. This is truly a significant historical event.

Amber and Mannix had spoken with the leaders of The Enchanted over multiple video chats. Madame Secretary was also involved with two of her senior staff. Secrecy is paramount and this was reiterated multiple times during these chats. In the weeks after these meetings, these leaders were invited to attend in person without too much fanfare so as to attract attention. This plan was too important and it must go ahead without any glitches.

Mannix stands at the lectern, adjusting the microphone. His voice, steady and clear, carries through the large, austere room.

"Thank you all for being here today to hear about '*Operation Enchantment*'. On behalf of Amber and myself, we extend a heartfelt welcome. And especially to the Enchanters who have travelled great distances to stand with us. Your presence here is not just an honour, it is a symbol of resilience and for a world united once more.

"Operation Enchantment is about us gathering together to honour a legacy, an enchanted legacy. Our history is one etched with suffering and the near eradication of our people during the wars. Entire generations lost. Entire lineages broken. Yet, we endure. And that endurance is thanks to the wisdom and courage of the few Enchanters who chose to conceal their magic, to protect what remained of our kind. It is because of their vision, that we are here today." He pauses as the audience gives him appreciative applause. "I thank you, but we are not here as survivors, we are here as a people reclaiming our future. It is time we became part of the greater human race again."

He pauses as his emotions come to the fore. Breathing deeply he continues, "Our plan is taking shape and with the help of everyone in this room, we will show society how The Enchantment Community will bring about change and provide positive contributions. The rumours and innuendo will be disparaged, all humans, magical or not, will live together in peace again." He pauses once more due to light applause. "Thank you, I will hand over to Amber now who will explain how all of this will happen."

Amber stands as the applause continues for Mannix and herself. Mannix takes a seat where Amber had been seated and angles himself towards her at the lectern. They are a team, a team that is making history and he wants everyone to know this.

"I am overwhelmed to see you all here. It has been a long two years of careful planning to reach this point in Operation Enchantment, a place where it is becoming apparent we Enchanters will be accepted again. So, how do we do this? Well, we will use our magic for good with the following ideas being only the beginning of what can be done." She turns to a video screen with ideas in point form and begins reading while using a pointer.

"Our enchantments will help heal our environment – bring fresh, clean water to all communities, show how to grow food sustainably, improve and upgrade tech, and raise funds to enhance our TRAI community so they may continue to keep everyone safe." Amber waits as the clapping slows, then continues, "We will help to solve issues like disease outbreaks, deal with rogue robots or more terrorists, and in the event of natural disasters, we will work with scientists using a mix of magic and tech to manage the impact. The Enchantment Community will be seen as an asset and no longer be considered a threat."

My circuits buzz with excitement and I am as proud of Amber as I am of Mannix. She has a determination to get things done, something I had seen and felt when we first met. All this is strengthening my desire to help the Enchanters become one with humanity, to be of use like we, the TRAI community, has been. I will use this strength to bring about this change, a change that has been too long in happening.

# NINETEEN

Mannix

3040 - The Secret is Out

OPERATION ENCHANTMENT HAS REACHED a point where our secret society can finally show its face. No more hiding, no more being ashamed, and no more being embarrassed of our powers.

We planned the announcement to be from The Nichols Centre room where our many meetings had been held. This time the world's media was invited to cover The Enchantment Community 'coming out' and rejoining society. The date of June 30 was set, an auspicious date because this is when all the terrorist wars ended. The Peace Treaty was signed in what was then Rome in 2950. By late 2970s, the terrorist enclaves were well into their campaigns, which had started during the war years, so that Treaty was only in force for under thirty years.

Amber and I are at the lectern, which is adorned with the movement's logo and around the room we have flags, banners and brochures, all indicating how much 'Operation Enchantment' is real. We tell them about how we have helped Harbour City already and our vision for the future. Both Amber and I speak from our hearts, which we hope conveys how much we want this plan to work.

Questions are thrown at us from journalists, influencers and television hosts. One journalist yells from the back of the room, "Hello, I'm Steven Popple from the Good Morning Show and I'm sceptical. You say you will 'heal our environment, teach people how to grow food sustainably, improve and upgrade tech' and more. Just how do you two young things and your small team plan to do these worthwhile things? Where is the money for all this? How is our fractured world going to manage such things?"

We field questions like these with caution making sure our message is clear and the public will learn to trust us Enchanters, we are not what the terrorists had painted us – bumbling fools where our magic caused trouble and chaos.

This journalist is not from our local TV station and with the clothes he's wearing, I know he is not from our city, his attire is casual and bright, not something our citizens would wear. He is the first of the international media to speak.

I answer him trying to calm the mutterings in the room, "Thank you for your question, Steve. We have been working quietly on Operation Enchantment for five years. Gathering our strengths, raising funds via our community and we have been promised grants by various governments. Yes, our world is fractured and this is exactly what our movement is about, we come together to make our world safer, more prosperous and be about pooling our resources for the common good. We may be young, but our community has people of all ages helping this cause. Give us a chance to prove ourselves and help us to heal the world's differences."

The journalist continues, "Hmm, that is admirable and our world, or what is left of it, needs help to recover. Five years is a long time to be working on one project, I feel the citizens of the world will be expecting much of your organisation."

"We hope to help where we are able, Steve, no country will be left alone with their struggles. Thank you for your questions, anyone else?"

We field questions for another half an hour but it is the last question from a young journalist that makes quite an impact. She stands, "Delia Artemus from the Sporades Archipelago, Greece. Her accent lilts over what is now a quiet room as everyone turns towards the back of the room. "You've spoken about helping Harbour City and its surrounds," she says, speaking confidently while addressing the whole room. "But what about the smaller nations - those left without resources or leaders? How will the Enchanters help them survive?"

A hush follows.

Amber glances at me before replying. "The world isn't divided by borders anymore. What's left of it is connected by survival. Our goal isn't to rebuild empires, it's to restore balance. We'll start by sharing what we've learned: healing the land, clearing the terrorist zones, stabilising climates where we can."

I add, "We're also training new guardians... people, not just Enchanters, to use small spells for everyday rebuilding. Food growth, clean water, communication networks. Magic won't replace hard work, but it can give smaller communities a fighting chance, in fact, all of us a fighting chance."

The journalist nods slowly. "So... no politics, only cooperation?"

"Exactly," Amber replies with a wide smile. "The age of domination is over. Those of us who are left owe it to future generations to have a world where all beings are safe and live comfortable lives. The Enchanters along with the TRAI community will work together to achieve this for all of the countries left, no matter their size.

Applause erupts. A standing ovation. The sound is deafening as I place my arm around Amber's shoulders and we both raise our arms waving them for all to see. Madame Secretary is next to us now and thanks us then addresses the media thanking them for their time too.

Three hours later the room has emptied except for Toria, Travis, Amber's parents and a select number of Enchanters.

"Oh I am glad that's over." Amber places her head on my chest as I nod in agreement. "I am wiped."

Toria hugs us both. "Congratulations, you've done it. Operation Enchantment is out in the world."

"Yes, and we're so proud of what you have achieved." This from Amber's parents.

"Thanks Toria. Thanks Mr and Mrs Sarkington. We couldn't have done this without your help and the help of the Enchanter and TRAI communities."

"This was your idea, Mannix. You put in the groundwork to help make The Enchantment Community accepted again. Yours and Amber's work." Mr Sarkington's face beams with immense pride as he places his hands on our shoulders.

I look at all of them as they each show us their love and support, it's overwhelming. "Amber and I are so lucky to have had this help, your help. But let's not get ahead of ourselves, we have only made an announcement so far, we are yet to prove ourselves. As that journalist said, he is sceptical, and I'm sure many others are too. We also have the smaller countries to consider as the Greek journalist pointed out."

Toria turns towards us both, "Don't undersell yourselves. Take pride with what you have achieved so far. You are the change we have been waiting for. How I wish the Professor was here to see this." She hangs her head, I know she still misses him every day. She has told me of her feelings and of the secret 'human' programming the professor had installed in her system, but this is Toria's strength, her empathy towards humans, and me especially, gives her a power no other TRAI has.

I have unwittingly become a symbol for change with Amber beside me, who is seen as the catalyst for all Enchanters to come forward. Amber is the trusted one, I am the revered one. This, however, makes me uncomfortable, I am a mere human with some magical powers, I feel reverence does not fit with me. How have I earned this level of respect when I'm still in my twenties?

The announcement causes a stirring of pride amongst Enchanters. However, some remain quiet, not yet ready to expose themselves. These are elders who want to see the plan work before joining our cause. Amber and I do an exhausting round of interviews, where we end up defending our movement because of public protests, not everyone is pleased about our magic being used again. This was something we expected, but the extent of public negativity was not to be ignored.

Protests have been relatively small but their voices hit home to our citizens. Many, like the journalist from the morning show, are sceptical. We have much work to do to prove our worth. The smaller countries will certainly be looking for assistance, the young journalist's article had gone viral, although she did paint us in a good light.

I CALL an emergency meeting at The Nichols Centre. We need to quell the level of unrest before our movement is shattered and The Enchantment Community's quest is no more. We're all seated in a circle discussing the best way forward. Ideas are thrown around, many not really hitting their mark, but it is from an unexpected event that we receive the impetus needed to show our strengths.

Feral animals.

Since the terrorist enclaves were decimated and only a few families have chosen to still live in the Second Zone, the ferals have grown in numbers. There are not enough humans in the area to keep their numbers in check. Mutant kangaroos, emus and other birdlife, along with giant lizards, snakes, spiders, and insects begin to encroach on Harbour City. This is a new war we have to tackle.

Citizens are bitten by snakes and spiders, some bites are deadly. The two-headed kangaroos are as tall as robots and TRAI have their hands full when they try to defend citizens. There are now curfews in place, no one is allowed out alone during the early morning or any time after dusk. TRAI patrol the city and have been given orders to kill ferals within the city area. This is the time for The Enchantment Community to show how magic can help. Our aim is to draw the mutant ferals back to the Second Zone.

. . .

I AM SITTING on the lounge in my apartment thinking about what we are achieving after what has been nine months of continuous work on our part to keep our movement alive. Amber is in the kitchen. "I take it we need more spells calling the animals back to their environment."

She walks towards me. "I have sent messages to our community, Mannix. We need Enchanters who are able to lure the mutant animals back to where they belong. There will be Enchanters who know how to manipulate their senses luring them back. I'm brewing tea, would you like some?"

"No, I'm good, thanks." I think about these Enchanters who can do such things.

"How interesting? I look forward to seeing how that manipulation will work. I hope they come forward soon, we need to do something, we need a win." My anxiety about the public negativity against Enchanters has manifested in a rash covering my chest and it also wreaks havoc with my powers. I am now second guessing them.

Amber sits at the end of the lounge placing my legs on her lap. Her tea sits on the side table cooling. "This will work, it has to. Years of working towards a solution on how to unite everyone will not go to waste." She picks up her tea and sips. "Ah, nothing like a tea to put everything into focus."

"If only everything was easy to solve by drinking tea. We also need to cull the number of ferals, they have tripled in these five years. The citizens of our our city are traumatised, especially the children." As I say this we hear screams from the park across the road. We both jump up into action. I message Toria and Travis in case we need assistance.

We arrive at the same time to see a baby black snake, only a metre in length. It is cut in half and there are two children crouched behind a sapling tree that is doing nothing to hide them. I walk slowly towards them, not wanting to alarm them. "We're here to help. Tell me what happened?"

The girl, who is the older of the two, speaks. "We were walking home, our sports bus dropped us off. We only live over there." She points towards a block of apartments next to where I live. "Then this snake was in front of us, hissing so loud my ears hurt. My skin crawled with fear. I was shaking, scared for both of us. My brother let go of my hand and found a stick in the bushes. He kept smashing at the snake who was slashing its head back and forth." She begins to cry, her little brother now leaning into her.

"Thank you for telling us your story, you were both very brave. Would you like to go home now?" I thought about the snake hissing, I had heard many of them in The Second Zone and remember my ears hurting too. And this snake was only a baby.

"Yes please," she sniffles.

"I'll take them Mannix," says Amber. "Come with me you two, I'll make sure you make it home safe."

Toria and Travis both walk towards me. Toria says, "These two were lucky this snake wasn't fully grown. Still, a metre long is still dangerous. This is a dire situation, other children have been maimed or killed just this week. We need to do more, Mannix."

"What about poison?" Travis asks.

"It's an idea but we must be careful. Children, dogs and cats may inadvertently be exposed to the poisons too."

"That's right Toria, it was one of the ideas thrown around. Amber and I were discussing the possibility of The Enchantment Community doing something, it will help our cause." I explain Amber's idea of luring the ferals back to the Second Zone.

They both look at each other. Toria is impressed. "That's interesting. Sounds like a top idea if it works."

"I hope it will, but Amber only sent the messages an hour ago, no responses yet. And, manipulating the ferals to head back to their environment is the best idea we have at the moment."

"You'll receive responses later tonight or maybe tomorrow morning, I am sure Enchanters will reply. For now Travis and I will organise to get rid of the snake, we don't want any other ferals attracted to it and help themselves to dinner."

I thank them and head back home, maybe I will have a tea now.

I AWAKE the next morning to a message from Amber, Enchanters have answered. Enough of them to make this idea work. I call her while still in bed.

"So how many answered?"

"Twenty people, all with different strengths. One Enchanter even knows how to keep the ferals from entering the city. She can place a spell around the city's perimeter to stop them entering. It's all part of Geomancy magic, a few others have some skills in this too. She is also willing to teach other Enchanters like you and I how to do this so we can teach others around the world."

"Amber, this is great. With the help of these Enchanters and their skills, we will put a stop to the protests and The Enchantment Community will be accepted fully again."

We continue talking until it's time for me to get myself

ready and meet her at The Nichols Centre. We have work to do.

# TWENTY

Toria

The Last Vial

I PICK IT UP GINGERLY. This tiny vial is the last one left. The other two have helped to keep my ageing system going for the past five years. I hold it up to the light, it is as blue as the day I received this amazing gift. As I add it to my system, I think if I have another few years of feeling at my optimum for my age, then I am happy.

My concerns for Mannix and Amber have pushed me to use this last vial. I need my strength to help them with this war we are fighting against the ferals. And to stop the protests against the Enchanters being part of our world again. We TRAI are not affected by the ferals although the kangaroos are a challenge. When we are in a fight with the larger ones of them, especially a male one, there is every chance we will be hurt. We have lost a few TRAI along the way.

I remember many scuffles while on missions in the

Second Zone. One incident gave me cause to fear for any humans who encounter a crazed kangaroo. A colleague spotted one roaring towards him, I was a few metres away and ran to help when I realised he was in trouble. By the time I reached him, the kangaroo had torn him to shreds, metal strewn throughout the bush path. It took only minutes for this to happen, it is something I told all TRAI to be wary of.

I sit heavily in my favourite lounge chair, the one from the Professor's home. The leather is weathered and soft, making it even more comfortable. When I sit here, I feel closer to him. What would he think of the public's opinion against the Enchanters? I'm sure he would be disappointed. "Professor, would you send us some luck from wherever you are? The Enchantment Community need to be part of society, our world needs to be united as one. Is peace that elusive?"

In his lifetime he never really saw peace. The world was only at peace for a short time before the terrorists began their reign of terror. If he had, I would not have been designed and built. Should I be thankful to the terrorists? No, I don't think so, another threat like the ferals would have necessitated us TRAI to be built.

I feel the blue liquid working its magic, my system gaining more strength. I will need all the strength I have left to help rid the city of ferals.

I stand and head towards my front door, it's time to attend another birthday celebration.

ARRIVING AT THE BARRACKS, I find Travis is standing out the front of Amber's home. "Good timing, were you waiting for me?"

"Affirmative. I sensed you were close."

Travis has always spoken with a robotic voice, I guess the Professor only programmed me to talk with a more human sound. All part of his plan, I guess. I am grateful he chose me to be the empath, a robot with human feelings.

We're welcomed inside the Sarkington's home by Amber. Each year we come together for birthdays, this time Jon's birthday is being celebrated. Today he is thirty-eight.

The joy I feel at these events gives me the sense of being part of a family. Something a robot would never need to feel, but for me, it is a pleasure and I am humbled to be allowed into this close knit family.

"Hi Toria, hey Travis. We have good news." Mannix says this as we all make ourselves comfortable around the dining table. Jon is looking better now, he has had some serious health issues lately.

There is silence. "Well, are you going to tell us what it is?"

"I'm working in some drama, Toria." A drum roll ensues.

"Get on with it, Mannix or I will tell them."

"Well, it was your doing, Amber. But seeing as I have started, I'll keep going ... we have had twenty Enchanters respond, they know how to perform Geomancy magic. This is how we are going to lure the ferals back home."

"That's wonderful news. This is a double celebration now." I watch as Travis opens a bottle of bubbly, something I wish we could enjoy, my circuits are mesmerised by the popping fizz.

We discuss how Geomancy magic works by manipulating the homelands to call animals back. Flowers and plants bloom in familiar patterns as the terrain leading out of the city reshapes guiding the ferals home. They are lured by the attractions to the altered terrain as it mimics their natural surrounds. The Enchanters will work their magic using trees to bend towards the right path and this path lights up with bioluminescent moss visible only to the ferals.

"Will all the ferals within the city be lured?"

"This is where we Enchanters come in, Toria. It is up to us to enhance the Geomancy so no ferals are left behind," explains Amber.

I stand clapping with pride, "This is fantastic. It is what we have been waiting for. The Enchanters will have this win and our world will be at peace."

"This is our hope," replies Mannix. "And it will be up to us to keep the ferals where they belong. One Enchanter has shown us a spell on how to keep the ferals in their terrain and not enter the city. So, Amber and I along with other Enchanters willing to join us, will travel the world showing other countries how to keep their feral numbers down and out of their cities.

"This is wonderful, but how will the feral numbers be controlled?"

Amber answers me, "Keeping them in their terrain means they will feed on each other, Mother Nature will do her job in keeping numbers down. If for some reason, numbers grow again, we Enchanters will give Mother Nature a helping hand."

"You have everything under control," I say clapping. Jon smiles and claps along with me.

# TWENTY-ONE

Mannix
A United World

WITH THE SUN BARELY RISEN, the outer districts of Harbour City are quiet for now, citizens are still in deep slumber.

A low hum beckons, Mother Nature herself is whispering, vibrating around us. Amber and I stand with our army of Enchanters, we have grown to more than two thousand, in formation on the city's southern edge, cloaked in soil-toned robes stitched with symbols of our ancient power. After over five years of planning, training, and waiting, we are ready to return as guardians for a world needing to be united.

Toria and her TRAI watch on behind us, her metal body in readiness for what may be her last challenge. The feral mutant kangaroos, tusked lizards, giant snakes, airborne and crawling insects are like a living tide, many of the animals severely disfigured and unrecognisable from their original form. Born from the poisoned wilds of the Second Zone and similar areas around the world, as well as the toxic mess left after too many years of war, they had overrun entire areas of the city. Now, they are paused sensing a shift.

The cicadas' song is silenced by Mother Nature's call. She has set this momentous operation in motion with us her aides.

We Enchanters raise our hands in unison. With our voices melding into a chant pulsing like a heartbeat. Our geomancy spell has begun. Trees bend, paths beckon and the bioluminescent moss draws the ferals to the city outskirts.

Mother Nature continues intoning her low hum enticing the ferals to follow. This allows us to leave the city following the ferals as they head towards the Second Zone. Toria and her team behind us are in readiness for any problems.

Our magic carries the memory of the history of our people. Our ancestors are with us today ensuring our success.

Many of the ferals are entranced as the rhythm of the Earth lulls them into calm. Each species follows the other, a mesmerised group heeding their destiny. I step forward, coaxing the snarling kangaroos to whimper and obey me as I utter a single word, *"home"*, then guide them back through the Second Zone towards the bush and the arid beyond.

Some ferals do not obey and this is when Toria and her TRAI take over. If these animals have mutated to the point where nothing, not even magic works on them, then they are destined to be destroyed.

The sun is well overhead warming us. We watch on as

the last of the ferals head towards the Second Zone, the bush just outside our city is quiet once more.

Amber is the first to speak. "I am overwhelmed with relief. We did it!"

Cheers come from us Enchanters and the TRAI.

"We did, Amber. With our army of Enchanters and our beloved TRAI team, our combined magic and strength has rid Harbour City of ferals." I say this with pride and a feeling of great achievement.

We all hug each other with sighs of relief and understanding of what we have achieved. "The world will be reunited as one. Terrorists, what is left of them, will fear us and think twice before attacking. Every town and city left in our world will benefit from what we have learned, we will help them. With the ferals where they belong, we will be able to control their numbers and keep them out of our cities. I, Mannix, will no longer hide my magic. The Enchanters are back."

THE PEOPLE OF HARBOUR CITY, afraid to be outdoors for the past too many years, now line the streets, their cheers swelling like a storm. We Enchanters file back into the city with the TRAI. My heart swells and all the doubts that had befallen me lift from my shoulders and disappear.

Madame Secretary, her team and many other distinguished citizens are waiting for us in front of the Professor's statue. I fall back and wait for Toria, I need her by my side as we hear what Madame Secretary has to say. When she reaches me, I simply bow my head then lift my head to give her a beaming smile as I look up.

"We did it," she whispers.

I take her hand as we walk towards Madame Secretary where Amber is waiting for us. The three of us stand together and listen.

"Citizens of Harbour City, today we are free. Free from the terrorists, free from the ferals." She stops as the crowd bellows with cheers, whistles and clapping. As the noise quietens, she continues. "It is with great gratitude we welcome these heroes, our TRAI and The Enchanters, who together have set us free." The cheers erupt again.

Madame Secretary continues outlining what this means not only for the city but for our world. We will now be one people united in a peaceful world. She explains how Amber and I, along with The Enchanters who helped us today, will travel the world to help others achieve what we have done. Help these countries to rid themselves of terrorists and contain any feral animals they may have been dealing with. "These young people are our future, it is important we all remember this day. To our TRAI, Mannix and Amber and your fellow Enchanters, we are in your debt." She pauses for effect while the crowd cheers once more. "Thank you all," she says as the crowd calms again, "it is time we all go on with our day and know our city is now safe and secure."

As the crowd disperses, Madame Secretary invites us all into The Nichols Centre. "Follow us, all of you," she indicates to her team and dignitaries, "let us head into the common room for more celebrations."

The common room is a burst of colour with our photos projected onto the screen, balloons covering the ceiling; some small, some big in gold and silver, floating above us. Travis playfully hits a few as we watch them scatter and float to another spot.

"You big lug, who knew you had a playful side." He gives me a nod and keeps playing with the balloons.

"This is amazing! To see all of these Enchanters here, it is a dream come true."

"It is, Amber. And it's all for us – the TRAI, The Enchanters and everyone who has helped us achieve peace." She gives me a huge smile and my heart melts knowing we are safe now and ready to see what our future holds.

Music takes me out of my reverie as waitstaff mingle amongst us offering hors d'oeuvres and drinks. I realise my stomach has been gurgling so I take a few morsels, stuffing them in my mouth.

Madame Secretary walks towards us. "Enjoy your party, all of you. We are most proud of your achievements, and I for one, look forward to how you will be able to implement these strategies in the countries you will be visiting. Now, I must leave and continue my duties elsewhere, stay and enjoy the rest of the afternoon and evening."

I take her hand as she offers it and thank her. "A heartfelt thanks for your support in all of this, Madame Secretary. Please enjoy the rest of your day."

"Thank you Mannix. I will be in touch soon to discuss your travel plans and what you require my government to help you with."

We watch on as she leaves the room. A huge sigh escapes me.

"Are you ok, Mannix?"

"I am Toria. I guess the gravity of the situation has finally hit me, so many things could have gone wrong, but we have emerged victorious. This is huge for me, for all of us."

"Of course, we all have much to be grateful for. Now, I think it may be time for us to enjoy this party, what do you think?"

I give a loud whoop and we all head to the dance floor.

IN THE QUIET of my apartment, Toria, Travis, Amber and I are reflecting on the past almost ten years.

"I am thirty next month. This is a number I never thought I would reach. If it wasn't for both of you, Toria and Travis, who rescued me as a rebel teen in the Second Zone, I would not be here today."

Amber, who is seated next to me on the lounge, smiles. "I am so glad you were rescued, Mannix. You have been the catalyst for change, for bringing The Enchanted back into the fold and for bringing peace to our world. And I love you for it."

A huge rush of red floods my face as I kiss Amber's cheek. "I am humbled you think I did this on my own, without you all it would not have been possible." I whisper 'I love you too' in her ear.

She beams placing her hand on my face, giving me a loving stroke. "We are a team, Mannix, you are right. But it is your leadership that has brought us to this point. I, for one, am very grateful to know you."

Travis also responds, "Affirmative. I agree. With our combined skills, we have achieved what many wanted."

We continue talking until after midnight when Toria and Travis finally say goodbye. I turn to Amber, "I don't know about you but I am wiped. I think I'm going to sleep for days." I take her hand bringing it to my lips and with this gentle kiss and both smiling, we walk back to my apartment.

# TWENTY-TWO

## Mannix and Amber
### Let the Travels Begin

AMBER and I leave with a small crew of TRAI to travel to the countries who have requested our help. This mission will take time and we give it all we can. Even though we call them missions, it is the TRAI who protect us when we encounter ferals. We are the delegates sent to meet with other Enchanters and convince them to become part of society again. We have succeeded in many countries and we are in our last city for one more mission and then looking forward to heading home soon.

Of all the countries we had visited to meet with Enchanters and help eradicate ferals, it was Hudson City that needed our help the most. Not only did the mutant bears cause anguish, but the Orca population had mutated to an even fiercer hunter, its feeding frenzies were the cause of the seas being stripped bare of many edible fish species. We met with environmental scientists to help devise a plan of how to minimise their effect. After a plan of attack was formed, we headed to our next mission.

I pull my jacket tighter, not because of the cold, but because Amber wasn't standing beside me.

She is ahead of me again. She always is when she senses danger is close.

Amber had detected feral bear noises and asked the TRAI to head towards the sounds. I find myself watching the way she tilts her head as she scans the horizon. She is precise, alert, impossibly calm. We have both become accustomed to how these missions play out. We were not meant to be so involved in these missions, but it is just the way things have played out. We were careful to use the TRAI and keep ourselves safe.

"Anything?" I call out to her as I head closer.

Amber glances back towards me. "They are not far, can you hear their growls?"

We have been travelling for six months. Long enough for silences between us to stop feeling awkward. Long enough for me to know the sound of her footsteps, the rhythm of her movements, the way she always positioned herself between me and the world, always in protection mode. Even though we have been a couple for years now, it was this trip that had cemented our relationship.

She places her hand up to stop me moving closer, but I go to her side anyway. Using her transcoder, she orders the TRAI to wait on the outskirts of the coastal enclave.

I can feel Amber's anxiety. "We're not alone."

My heart kicks hard against my ribs. "Ferals? Are they bears?"

"Yes." She pauses, then added quietly, "Look over there," she points. "Stay close."

She doesn't need to say it. But we always say it to each other anyway.

We arrive where the TRAIs had stopped. The lead one telling us to look towards a clearing, "Two ferals are guarding the door to the cabin."

We acknowledge and ask him to send TRAI to remove them from the entrance. We watch on as this happens. The bears didn't know what hit them as the TRAI perform their duty with efficiency. We head towards the front door with TRAI ahead protecting us.

They slam the door open. Amber ushers them in and follows with me close behind. The feral screeches tear through the air as they surge forward. We are in luck, there are only three more of them.

I indicate to Amber we head towards the survivors huddled nearby – young Enchanters, fear written across their faces. We assure them of their safety as the TRAI deal with the feral bears. They watch on with the fear dissipating as the TRAI handle the bears easily.

Amber bends down removing the ropes binding the three of them together. "How were you captured?"

The taller male tells her how they had been out hunting when the bears had appeared. "We are recreational hunters and seek out ferals to help keep numbers down. We were caught out this time."

"You are safe now, I am Amber and this is Mannix. We will have you transported to a hospital in the city, you're going to be ok."

"Thank you, we know who you are. Your reputation, along with that of the TRAI, is well-known."

She looks at me with pride flooding her face.

I am happy this is our last mission, we are heading home at the end of the week.

When the Enchanters are out of the cabin, we head back to our vehicles and begin our journey back to Hudson City. "Amber, we did it. Tomorrow we can go to city hall and leave our journals with the mayor. We can head home knowing we have done what we set out to do."

Our eyes meet. Love flows between us.

Back at our hotel, showered and full from the room service dinner, weare relaxing on the bed.

For a moment, the world feels small. It is just the two of us.

I lean towards her, my hand caressing her cheek. She lifts her head allowing me to kiss her. We come together, the adrenaline of our missions giving way to our passion.

# TWENTY-THREE

Toria

The world has grown quieter. Peace is around us and is within us all.

Harbour City is quieter as its citizens go about their business without the fear and uncertainty that gripped them during the years of war and the past twenty years. There has been much healing but more healing needs to be done, for everyone the world over. We have embraced this new peace and it has held.

Further healing will take time, years even. We TRAI are here to ensure this peace is not broken and along with The Enchanters we will guard the citizens of Harbour City without alarming them. They now have a future very different from previous years and although they will never forget our troubled past, it is the peace that will be protected above all.

Children now play without looking over their shoulders or fear of being ravaged by ferals, and The Enchanters with their magic, once hidden, are part of society, accepted. Their magic is there if needed, it's in the background as are we TRAI. Citizens see us as their protectors and we TRAI especially, will remain vigilant without causing fright and fear.

SITTING beneath an ancient fig tree near the harbour, sunlight gleaming on the metal of my arms, my movements are slower now. The gentle tremor in my fingers is no longer a sign of caution but of wear.

I feel it, something deep inside my circuits. Not pain exactly, but a kind of weakening. It takes longer for me to sort memory threads, and sometimes my voice catches when I'm uncertain what to say, words come fleetingly and without form. A few of my systems had begun to fail in quiet, dignified ways. The optimised lens in my left eye no longer aligns. My auditory sensors sometimes confuse bird-song or cat wails with distant alarms. But I don't mind. Not anymore.

Mannix and Amber, along with a team of TRAI, visited many cities teaching what we had all learned. This has helped the fragile peace to strengthen as smaller countries were also included. Their mission was long and protracted but successful. They have been home for some time.

Mannix visits often, bringing me oil I no longer need and telling me stories I love to hear. How he and Amber are doing, her parents and brother. His adopted family. He tells me how he is now 'home', something he has never had.

His stature is now older, he is steadier and stands proud. His happiness is apparent and he wears it with love and gratitude. He calls me "Tori" now, a soft nickname making my circuits hum just a little brighter when he is with me.

"I think it's time," I told him the last time we were together, my voice low and even.

He had not argued. He simply nodded, took my hand, cold and metallic but still mine, and walked with me to the small shelter I'd helped build years before. It overlooks the sea, is eco-friendly and powered by solar. It is filled with many TRAI memories. A shelter for all ageing TRAI.

Time passes slowly as my body does what it has to do. I think of Mannix and the last time we were together, only three days ago. He wanted to stay with me but I told him this is something a TRAI does on their own. This is my time.

There, in the stillness of a twilight sky, I prepare for rest. My systems are powering down one by one, not in failure, but in peace. I had uploaded my final logs to the city's archive: thoughts on hope, on humanity, on change, on choice. I quietly thank the Professor, my father whose love I felt but had not known how to return it, for bringing me into this world and giving me the power of human feelings.

My last thought is of the boy in the Second Zone, and the moment I first felt something close to love.

THE END

# ACKNOWLEDGMENTS

This story, *The Robot's Heart: Toria's Story*, is a novella where I wanted to highlight the perils of climate change along with what is happening around the Artificial Intelligence (AI) space.

If we do nothing about halting climate change there will be consequences. Will we have ferals to contend with in the future? Science Fantasy stories are about what may happen, about what our future may look like if we neglect our planet. Humans should not allow the demise of our planet nor the immoral use of AI, especially not stealing from creatives.

I wanted Toria's story to give readers a hopeful sense of our future as we rely more heavily on machines, robots and AI. Will scientists be able to give humans the tools to use these things responsibly, or is there a world where robots and AI take over?

I'd like to thank everyone who has helped me with this book, especially Conchita GarSantiago who read early drafts and Mark Drolc for yet another fabulous book cover. Thank you as always to my family and my friends, you are there for me whenever I need you.

And lastly, to everyone who has bought, read and reviewed my stories, I am happy you enjoy my work, an author without readers is very lonely. I appreciate your thoughts and I hope my stories keep you entertained for many years to come.

Happy reading,
Maria P Frino

# ABOUT THE AUTHOR

Maria has made a career of using words to communicate. Working at a TV station, her first paid job, nurtured Maria's love of words. A move to Sydney to study Communications gave her the opportunity to work with advertising & public relations agencies, corporate companies and newspapers. She has written PR, ads and newsletters for products from food to jewellery, fashion and interiors as well as garden and building products. When she is not writing corporate communications or as a Senior Reviewer for the online site, Weekend Notes, she works on her short stories, novellas and novels.

Her first published story, *The Studio* is a crime short story. *Xenure Station: A Billion Light Years,* is Maria's second short story. Both are available as eBooks online.

*The Decision They Made,* Maria's debut novel and her other books are available on her website – www.mariapfrino.com and many online sites, libraries and book shops. Buy these books as eBooks or print.

*Weaving Words,* an anthology Maria collaborated on, is also available as an audiobook. Maria contributed two short stories to this anthology along with eight other authors.

Her contemporary novel, *Fame & Other Disasters* is available as an ebook, in print version or as an audiobook.

Along with several other authors, Maria helped to establish ***Sydney Authors Inked,*** a collective of self-published authors who do author events. We discuss books, reading, publishing, and all book-related topics. Follow us on our website to find out where our events are held regularly. Anyone interested in books, writing and publishing is welcome to attend, look out for tickets on Humanitix or Eventbrite ticketing sites.

## ALSO BY MARIA P FRINO

The Decision They Made

Fame & Other Disasters

Edward's Cat

Xenure Station Trilogy

www.ingramcontent.com/pod-product-compliance
Lightning Source LLC
LaVergne TN
LVHW010625100826
845148LV00014B/3113

* 9 7 8 0 6 4 8 8 9 4 6 7 4 *